SNOWBOUND!

KEVIN MILLER

MILLIGAN CREEK
www.bakkenbooks.com

Cover illustration by Kierston Vande Kraats

ISBN 978-1-955657-64-8
For Worldwide Distribution
Printed in the U.S.A.

BAKKEN BOOKS

Published by Bakken Books
2023

Dedication

For Glenn and Donna Brown, Alvin Brown, and Lyle Block, who made the best snow maze ever!

Contents

1

Whiteout

Ribbons of snow streamed across the highway, driven by a savage wind. The navy-blue 1971 Plymouth Fury III station wagon's feeble headlights barely pierced the curtain of blowing flakes to illuminate the darkness beyond. When the driver switched his headlights to bright, they highlighted the snow rather than the road, and he quickly turned them back to dim. Struggling to see, he leaned over the aging vehicle's cold, cracked steering wheel as he peered at the yellow lane stripes emerging one after the other from the gloom.

"Stupid defrost!" he muttered as he used a soaking wet piece of paper towel to rub the fog off the inside of his windshield. The driver, twenty-five-year-old Dewey Biggs, had picked up the paper towel at his last stop, a gas station about fifty miles back in one of the dozens of small towns that littered the highway between Winnipeg and Saskatoon. That was also around the time his heater fan had stopped working. He knew he should have rented a car for this job rather than pick up a clunker from a second-hand dealer. But his boss, Earl, had been insistent on that point. Paying cash for a beater and then stealing the license plates off another vehicle and putting them on the Fury meant there was no way the station wagon could be traced back to Dewey after he ditched it. And Dewey couldn't wait to ditch it, though not literally, of course.

He had been driving for hours, but due to the near-whiteout conditions, he had only been able to travel at half the speed limit, which meant a trip that was supposed to take eight hours would take nearly twice that long. He'd tried calling Earl from a payphone back at the gas station to suggest he rent a motel room and wait for the storm to pass, but Earl hadn't answered, which wasn't unusual. Besides, Dewey already knew what his response would be. Earl was never one to wait, especially with so much riding on the outcome of this trip.

Despite his focus on the road, Dewey felt his head bob as sleep threatened to overtake him. He had no idea how he was going to keep this up all night. He shook his head to clear it. When that didn't work, he lowered his window and stuck his head out, hoping the cool night air would revive him. But the blowing snow stung his eyes, blinding him, and he quickly pulled his head back inside. When he pushed the button to roll his window back up though, it didn't respond.

"What the heck?" He stabbed the button repeatedly with his finger, but the window refused to budge. "Stupid freakin' thing!" Well, at least there was no worry about him falling asleep now; just freezing to death. Maybe in the next town he could get his hands on some cardboard and duct tape. He checked his watch. Yeah, right. At this hour, nothing would be open. He sighed—and shivered.

Just as sleep began to creep up on him again despite the blast of cold air and snow coming in his window, he caught sight of something in his rearview mirror. He did a double take and looked again. Nothing. Had he been dreaming? He rubbed his eyes and shook his head, then looked in the mirror one more time. There was no mistaking it. In the distance behind him was a pair of blue-and-red flashing lights. The police! How had they managed to find him? Had Earl ratted him out? Was that why he hadn't answered the phone?

Before he realized it, Dewey pressed his foot down on the accelerator, and the old station wagon surged ahead. Then he eased off slightly. There was no way he could outrun the police in that big blue boat, but what other option did he have?

He was so fixated on the lights behind him that he forgot to look where he was going and nearly swerved into the ditch, narrowly missing a big green road sign that said, "Milligan Creek 5." Catching himself just in time, he yanked on the steering wheel, causing the station wagon to slip into a fishtail.

"Whoa, whoa, whoa, whoa!" Dewey cried as the vehicle's considerable rear end swung back and forth across the slick highway, threatening to send him into a spin.

He got it under control just in time to see a gravel road to his left. He cranked the wheel and just made the turn. As he sped down the road, he turned off his headlights. He could barely see, but at least he couldn't be seen. Besides, back roads were notoriously straight in Saskatchewan, so he figured all he had to do was keep his hands locked on the steering wheel, and everything would be OK.

When he felt he was a safe distance from the highway, he let the station wagon roll to a stop, careful not to use his brakes in case his taillights gave him away.

As he sat and waited, a thought struck him. What if the police had seen him turn off the highway? What if they were creeping up on him right now, headlights off, so they could surprise him? He looked behind him. He couldn't see anything, but that didn't mean they weren't there. Then he looked in his back seat. There it was, the black hard-shell case at the heart of it all, the very thing that had caused him to embark on this perilous journey. If he managed to reach his destination, the case's contents promised to make him and Earl rich beyond their wildest imagination. Well, it would make Earl rich anyway, but Dewey would get his cut, and it would still be more money than he had ever seen before. However, if the police caught him with it now, not only would it mean the end of Dewey's dreams, it would also be the beginning of a nightmare—years spent in prison. There was no way he could risk that.

He grabbed the hard-shell case and opened his door. Huddling against the wind, he stood and looked around, but he could hardly see anything due to the darkness and the blowing snow. Should he risk his headlights? No, he would have to feel his way.

The instant he stepped off the road, he sank up to his hips in the snow.

"Dang it!" he cried, the wind tearing the words from his lips almost as quickly as they emerged. Using the case to hold himself up, Dewey extracted his leg and then stretched himself flat on the snow, spreading his weight out as much as possible, so he wouldn't sink.

As he slithered across the snow, eventually, he found himself going uphill. It wasn't what he expected, and it made the going all the harder, but he continued on. When he reached a barbed-wire fence, Dewey stopped, figuring it was as good a place as any. Using a red plastic ice scraper that he had bought back at the gas station, he began to dig.

After burying the case in the snow, he turned back toward the road and then paused. How would he know where to find the case when he returned? His mind raced, and then he reached into his jacket and pulled out the chain he wore around his neck. Dangling from it was a small gold padlock, a gift from his girlfriend, Amber, the last time he had gotten out of prison. It was one of a pair of matching padlocks. They had locked the other one to a bridge over the South Saskatchewan River in Saskatoon. Typically, when lovers did such a thing, they were supposed to throw away the key to symbolize their undying love, but for some reason Dewey had held onto it. He still wasn't sure if that's why he and Amber had broken up two weeks later or if it would have happened anyway, but now he was thankful for his decision.

Pulling the key from his pocket, he undid the padlock and then clipped it around the barbed-wire fence right above where the case was buried. Perfect. Not only would he know where to dig for it, if someone found the lock, they wouldn't know what it meant, and they wouldn't be able to remove it.

Once he made it back to the road, Dewey stood up and looked toward where the case was buried. The blowing snow had almost completely obliterated his tracks. Excellent. He got back in his car, narrowly avoided getting stuck in the ditch while he did a three-point turn, and then took off.

Only when he reached the highway did Dewey risk turning on his headlights again. Seeing no other vehicles, he wondered if the police had simply given up or if they had set up a roadblock for him a few miles ahead. He decided to check it out just to be sure. If the coast was clear, he'd return for the case and then resume his journey.

With the visibility improving slightly, Dewey had just gotten the station wagon up to speed when the heater fan kicked in. Amazing! He held his hand over the dashboard as the hot air poured out, a welcome contrast to the cold air blasting through his window. Maybe that was the trick: keeping the car above a certain speed. Now if only his window would work. He pressed the button and, voilà! It rolled back up! Believing his luck had finally turned around, Dewey decided to do the same. Maybe he had been imagining those police lights in his rearview mirror all along.

Cranking a U-turn, Dewey sped back down the highway to pick up the case. However, moments later, he saw flashing red-and-blue lights approaching. With no chance to get away, Dewey slowed down and drove as carefully as possible, not wanting to give the police any reason to pull him over.

But it wasn't the police; it was a snowplow. It roared past Dewey, sending up a shower of whirling snow that obliterated his view. Gripping the steering wheel with both hands, Dewey took his foot off the gas, allowing the station wagon to coast as he waited for the snow to clear.

When it did, he caught a flash of an eye and a huge set of moose antlers. And then Dewey's world went from white . . . to black.

2

Jumpers

The cold winter sun glistened off the sparkling white field, which seemed to stretch out forever beneath the bright blue dome of winter sky. Not a blemish marred the prairie landscape, save for a few sticks of faded yellow stubble poking up through the snow, and not a breath of wind stirred the air. The only sound came from a flock of English sparrows chirping as they whirled and swooped across the glistening, lung-freezing expanse. It was the picture of peace and tranquility, the perfect kind of day for—

VROOM!

The sparrows scattered as a black-and-silver Arctic Cat Jag snowmobile blasted over a small rise, throwing up a plume of snow as it tore across the field.

At the handlebars was fourteen-year-old Chad Taylor, his head concealed by a sparkling black helmet with a tinted full-face shield. Seated backwards behind him wearing a bright orange toque , a one-piece green denim snowsuit, and a pair of ski goggles was one of Chad's best friends, thirteen-year-old Andrew Loewen. He was acting as Chad's spotter. Extending behind the snowmobile was a multi-colored water ski tow rope. At the end of the rope was Matt Taylor, Chad's thirteen-year-old brother. Matt was strapped into a pair of downhill skis that the boys had picked up at a second-hand store that fall with precisely this sort of activity in mind, and he was having the time of his life.

"Faster!" Matt shouted, jabbing his right thumb into the air.

"He wants to go faster!" Andrew yelled over the roar of the machine.

"Faster, eh?" Chad said, glancing over his shoulder. "I can do that." He stood up and cranked a hard left, gunning the engine as he leaned into the turn. "Hang on!"

"You're supposed to warn me before you make the turn!" Andrew replied, gripping the snowmobile's rear bumper as he struggled to stay on board.

Taking advantage of the momentum, Matt swung out in a wide arc, nearly pulling the back end of the snowmobile with him as Chad pinned the throttle. His speed increasing due to his crack-the-whip motion, Matt aimed his skis at a huge ramp that the boys had built out of snow in the middle of the field. It was their first attempt at jumping it, and Matt wanted to make it spectacular.

Standing beside the ramp—which was nearly as tall as him—was thirteen-year-old Dean Muller, the fourth member of their tight-knit group. He was manning a video camera on a tripod, prepared to immortalize Matt's initial attempt.

As Matt bore down on the ramp, Dean checked the viewfinder to ensure his friend was in frame. "C'mon, Matt," he murmured. "You can do it."

His skis lined up perfectly with the jump, at the last second, Matt let go of the rope.

Across the field, Chad spun the snowmobile around,

so he and Andrew could watch Matt launch into the air in a breathtaking aerial display. A moment later, something flew into the air, all right, but it wasn't Matt.

The instant Matt hit the ramp, Dean was blinded by an explosion of snow that blasted him off his feet. When the flakes settled, he was flat on his back and covered in white stuff, the camera and tripod on top of him.

"Help!" a faint voice cried.

Dean spit the snow out of his mouth, wiped it off his face, and then sat up. "Just a minute!" After making sure the camera was OK, he jumped up and hurried over to Matt, who was half buried in what remained of the ramp, his arms and legs akimbo, one of his skis poking up out of the snow about three feet away from him.

"I guess we should have packed the jump a little better," Matt groaned as Dean unclipped his remaining ski, so Matt could finally straighten his leg.

"You think?" Dean said as he helped Matt to his feet. "You were supposed to go over the ramp, not through it."

"No kidding," Matt said, bending forward and sweeping the snow out of his hair.

Just then, Chad and Andrew roared up on the snowmobile. Chad killed the engine and flipped up his face shield. "Tell me you got that on film!"

Dean patted the camera. "In Technicolor. At least I think I did. I couldn't see a thing once the snow exploded in my face."

"Awesome!" Chad said. "I just wish you guys could have seen it from a distance. It was stunning!"

"We could always get him to do it again," Dean suggested, grinning as Matt shook the snow out of his jacket.

"Be my guest," Matt replied, straightening up and holding out the skis.

"Oh, no," Dean said, raising his hands as he stepped back. "You're the daredevil, not me."

"I don't mean the jump," Matt countered. "The skis. You're the only one who hasn't tried them yet."

"I don't know," Dean said, checking his watch. "It's getting kind of late."

"It's 2:30 in the afternoon," Andrew replied. "We have plenty of time." It was a Thursday, but the boys had gotten out of school early that day, as they would the following afternoon, due to parent/teacher interviews.

Dean glanced up at the pale winter sun and then eyed the skis uncertainly. "I don't know . . ."

"Come on," Matt said, resting his hand on Dean's shoulder as he bent over to unclip his ski boots. "Your feet are the same size as mine, right?"

"Yes, but—"

"No buts," Matt replied, wriggling out of one of the boots and shoving it into Dean's chest as he hopped on one foot. "You're going."

Minutes later, Dean was strapped into the skis and holding the tow rope, which was uncoiling slowly in front of him as Chad eased the snowmobile forward. When the rope went taut, it yanked Dean forward a few feet, nearly pulling him onto his face.

"Hey, wait!" Dean said. "I'm not ready!"

"Sorry!" Chad said. "Just need to make sure the rope is tight. Give me the signal when you're good to go!"

"And remember," Matt added, pulling off his ski goggles and putting them on Dean, "if you get in trouble, just let go of the rope."

"Got it," Dean replied, giving the goggles a final adjustment. He took a deep breath and then gave a thumbs-up to Andrew, who was spotting again. "Ready!" Dean said. "But take it slow!"

Andrew gave him a thumbs-up and then nudged Chad, who hit the gas. Dean lurched forward, bending over the skis and then leaning back. He continued to wobble back and forth like that until he regained his balance. "Hey, this isn't as hard as I thought," he said as Chad increased his speed slightly. Dean even began to cut back and forth a bit, skiing in and out of the snowmobile's track.

"That's how you do it!" Matt shouted, excited to see his timid friend spread his wings a bit. He had grabbed the video camera to film Dean's first attempt. "Keep going!" With one eye on the viewfinder, he gave Dean a thumbs-up as he circled past, and Dean returned the gesture.

"This is awesome!" Dean yelled.

Seeing Dean's thumbs-up and thinking it was directed at him, Andrew nudged Chad again. "He wants to go faster!"

"Hang on!" Chad said, revving the engine. "See how I warned you before I hit the gas this time?"

"Gee, thanks!" Andrew replied, gripping the rear bumper as the snowmobile surged ahead.

Dean lurched forward, pulled off balance by the unexpectedly rapid increase in speed. "Wait!" he shouted. "Slow down!" He tried to raise his hand to give a thumbs-down signal, but it took all his effort just to stay upright, and he was too terrified to let go of the rope. He began to swerve back and forth as he struggled to maintain his balance, riding first on one ski and then the other, sending up a huge spray of snow with each turn.

"Wow, he's a wild man!" Andrew said as he watched Dean's theatrics, thinking he was carving back and forth like that on purpose. "I never knew he had it in him!"

"Neither did I!" Chad said, looking back over his shoulder as he revved the engine even more. "Let's really give him a run for his money!" He cranked another hard turn.

"Heeeeellllpppp!" Dean cried as he whizzed past Matt on his next round.

"Let go of the rope!" Matt yelled as he ran after him.

"What?"

"The rope! Let go of the rope!"

Dean finally got the message and released the rope just as he reached the top of a small hill. He got at least a foot of air and disappeared over the other side.

Matt ran forward and crested the hill just in time to see Dean flailing his arms and yelling as he sped down the opposite slope, unable to stop.

"Oh no," Matt huffed, "he's heading straight for a . . ." He dropped the video camera and cupped his gloved hands over his mouth to amplify his voice. "Fence!"

3

The Gully

"Wow, that was incredible!" Matt said as Chad and Andrew roared up on the snowmobile, gliding to a stop beside him.

"What happened?" Andrew asked as he jumped off the machine.

"He must have got, like, ten feet of air!" Matt said.

Chad flipped up his visor. "What? How?"

"On that!" Matt said, pointing as he loped down the hill, struggling to run in the knee-deep snow. Chad and Andrew followed Dean's ski tracks with their eyes. They led straight toward a barbed-wire fence before veering sharply to the right, straight toward a round bale that had drifted over with snow. It formed a natural ski jump that had allowed Dean to clear the fence.

"Oh, man, I hope he's all right," Chad said, firing up the snowmobile. "Come on!"

Andrew hopped aboard, and they raced down the slope, passing Matt and then skidding to a stop beside the bale. Chad hit the kill switch and then vaulted off the machine and ran toward the fence, Andrew right on his heels.

"Dean!" Chad called, unable to see over the steep

drop-off into a gully on the other side of the fence. "Are you OK?"

"No!" Dean replied angrily.

"Oh boy," Chad said as he held down the top strand of barbed wire, so Andrew could clamber over it.

"What's the matter?" Matt asked as he ran up, huffing from his slog through the snow.

"I don't know!" Chad said, flopping over the fence.

When he and the other boys reached the edge of the drop-off, they didn't see anything at first, just some grey-and-black poplar trees poking up sporadically through the snow.

"What the heck?" Matt said, squinting as he panned the camera across the glistening, snow-filled gully.

"Dean, where are you?" Chad called.

"I'm right here!" Dean said, sounding even angrier.

"Where?" Chad asked.

"There!"

Matt directed the camera toward where Andrew was pointing and zoomed in. Sure enough, there was Dean—or at least part of him. All that was visible was his head sticking out of the snow. And he did not look happy. Unable to help himself, Matt nearly doubled over with laughter.

"It's not funny!" Dean said. "I can't even move my arms!"

"Can you feel your feet?" Andrew asked, scowling at Matt. "Knock it off," he whispered. "He could have really injured himself."

"No! I can't feel anything from the neck down!" Dean said, causing Matt to sober up in a hurry as he and the other boys exchanged worried looks.

"Should one of us get an ambulance?" Andrew asked.

"No! Just get me the heck out of here. I'm freezing!"

Matt, Chad, and Andrew bounded down the hill, which was nearly impossible in such deep snow. The gully was sheltered from the wind, so the snow hadn't hardened at all, and they sank up to their waists.

"Almost there," Chad grunted as he and the other boys essentially swam through the snow. When Chad finally reached Dean, his face was red—the parts of it that weren't covered by snow, that is. Even his goggles were filled with snow. Chad ripped them off and wiped Dean's face clean with his mitt.

"Don't move him!" Andrew said, sliding down beside Chad. "He might have a spinal cord injury!"

"I don't have a spinal cord injury!" Dean said as Matt showed up, camera rolling. "And get that camera out of my face!"

"How can you be sure?" Andrew asked. "You said you couldn't move your arms."

"Because they're pinned to my sides in the snow!" Dean replied. "Now dig me out of here before I turn into a Popsicle!"

As the other boys started to do exactly that—Andrew instructing them to be careful in case Dean really was hurt—Dean explained that when he hit the bale, it launched him so high into the air that he did a complete backflip. When he landed, he sank right up to his chin in the soft snow. And as far as he could tell, his feet were nowhere near the bottom.

They got his arms free quickly enough, but seeing as he was still clipped into the skis, the boys had to burrow down far enough to detach his boots. Once they were able to free Dean's feet, they could dig out the skis.

While Chad and Andrew continued to dig, Matt stood up and then flopped backwards, the snow forming a perfect lounge chair around him as he sat back to take in the view. "This place is incredible," he said. "How come we've never seen it before?"

"We have," Andrew said. "There's just never been this much snow." That winter had seen a near record snowfall, which meant Milligan Creek would likely be swollen more than ever come spring when the snow melted. However, despite their previous adventures canoeing that creek, the boys weren't even thinking about that yet. Winter still had way too much to offer. That was one of the joys of living in Saskatchewan. The prairies experienced four distinct seasons, each one with its own unique set of activities, and the boys made sure they maximized every opportunity for adventure that each season had to offer.

"You know what would be perfect here?" Matt asked.

"You helping us dig?" Chad said as he scooped out a mittful of snow and flung it at his brother.

"Y-yeah, c-come on, M-Matt," Dean said, his teeth chattering. "I'm n-not k-kidding about it being c-cold."

"Sorry about that." Matt rocked back and forth as he tried to stand up, unable to do so until Chad pulled him to his feet. "Anyway, as I was saying," Matt continued as he joined the other boys to help free Dean, "you know what would be perfect out here?"

"A 'No Trespassing' sign, seeing as we don't have permission to be on this side of the fence?" Andrew suggested.

"No," Matt said, the other boys' mockery failing to dampen his enthusiasm. "A snow fort. No, a snow fortress!"

Chad sat back on his haunches, puffing slightly from the exertion of digging, and surveyed the gully. He hated to admit it, but Matt was right. At the top of the ridge on the opposite side of the gully was a stand of trees. Throughout the winter, the trees had slowed the wind enough to cause it to deposit a huge volume of snow into the gully. Not only that, along the ridge was a massive outcrop of wind-hardened snow that curled over the edge, forming a hard cornice. It was a perfect snow tunneling location.

"Just think about it," Matt said. "A maze of tunnels, secret rooms, a trapdoor with a pit that people fall into but can't climb out of, a huge cave with a pillar in the center and beds carved into the walls where people can spend the night . . ."

"H-how d-do you b-build a t-trapdoor in a s-s-s-snow cave?" Dean asked, his teeth still chattering. By then the boys had nearly made it down to his feet.

"I don't know," Matt said, snow flying as he dug with both hands. "I'm just spitballing. But you get the idea." He paused and pointed. "Look at that side of the gully. We could tunnel in it for days. Heck, when we're done, we could even charge admission!"

"I don't know about that," Chad said. "We don't even know who owns this land."

"So we find out who does, get permission to dig here, and then give them a cut of what we earn," Matt replied.

"Got the first one," Andrew said, reaching down and pushing on the back of the ski binding, freeing Dean's right foot.

"Thank goodness," Dean said, wiggling his leg.

"See if you can use your foot to release the other binding," Andrew said. "There's also the liability issue," he added, glancing up at Matt, who paused to sound out the word "liability," counting the syllables on the fingers of his gloved hand.

"Five," Matt said. "Okay, I give up. What does 'liability' mean, Brainiac?"

"It means if someone got hurt—say if the snow cave

collapsed—who would be responsible?"

Matt scoffed. "I don't know. We can just get everyone to sign a waiver. The same thing we do when we go downhill skiing. Besides, if we build it right, it won't collapse."

"Sorry, I c-can't r-reach it," Dean said.

"Don't worry, I got you." Chad lay on his stomach and bent down to reach for the binding. "Almost got it—Aaggh!"

His cry was cut off as he fell headfirst into the hole they had dug around Dean, the soft snow collapsing around him.

"Grab his other leg before he suffocates!" Andrew cried as he grabbed Chad's left calf. Matt clutched Chad's right thigh, and they both heaved, falling back in the snow as Chad popped out of the hole.

"Thanks!" Chad said, spitting out snow and wiping it off his face.

"My foot's free!" Dean said, clambering out of the hole. "Finally."

They all looked down as the hole filled in behind him, completely burying the skis.

"The snow maze won't collapse, hey?" Chad said, giving his brother a skeptical look.

"Aw, shut up," Matt said, flinging snow at him. "And get digging, or we'll never find those skis."

4

The Mystery Patient

When Staff Sergeant Richard Romanowski passed through the front door of the Milligan Creek Hospital, his nose was met by a blast of the typical hospital smells—disinfectant, cleaning solution, and a whiff of a diaper that needed changing. But what really made his RCMP-issue mustache bristle was not the familiar smells but an unfamiliar sound that he rarely encountered inside of a hospital: giggling.

The laughter came from two teenage candy stripers peeking in the window of a patient's room just down the hall. Romanowski was about to ask them what was so funny when he was met by one of the town's two physicians, Dr. Bash Maharaj—at least that's who Romanowski thought it was.

The source of Romanowski's confusion was the fact that Bash had an identical twin, Harpreet, who served as Milligan Creek's other physician. The brothers had emigrated to Canada from India six months earlier. While the frigid winters of Saskatchewan were a sharp contrast to their subtropical home, they and their families had adapted quickly to small-town life on the prairies. This was made easier by the fact that both Saskatchewan and Punjab, the state where the brothers were raised, were known as the "breadbaskets" of their respective countries, each producing an abundance of wheat and other grains. The fact that Bash and Harpreet had grown up on a farm also helped to bridge the cultural gap between them and their prairie-dwelling patients.

The only complication was their status as identical twins. When locals talked about Dr. Maharaj or called to book an appointment, they always had to clarify which doctor they meant—Bash or Harpreet—which was no real burden. However, whenever people ran into the doctors on the street or in the hospital, as Romanowski had just done, their eyes tended to dart around as they looked for telltale signs that would help them differentiate one brother from the other. Even during an appointment, people were never quite sure they were being seen by the doctor they had requested, having to trust that the receptionist got it right.

Bash and Harpreet didn't make it any easier on the townspeople either. They styled their hair exactly the same way, even parting it on the same side, and they wore name tags on their white lab coats that merely said "Dr. Maharaj" instead of also including their first name or an initial. When they met people on the street, rather than clarify who they were at the outset, they tended to grin in silent amusement, either tired of having to explain who they were, thinking the locals should have figured out how to tell them apart by now, or secretly enjoying themselves as they watched people struggle.

As a police officer with enhanced detective skills, Staff Sergeant Romanowski prided himself on being able to tell the brothers apart with no more than a glance, but even he was prone to slip up from time to time. Perhaps due to the distraction created by the candy stripers, this was one of those times.

"Good morning, Doctor . . . Maharaj!" Romanowski said, speaking Bash's last name a little louder than normal, happy to have at least gotten that part right.

"Staff Sergeant Romanowski, so good to see you. I take it you're here to interview our mystery patient? He was unconscious all day yesterday, but he's finally come around."

"That I am," Romanowski replied, happy the doctor was eager to get down to business, so he could avoid the issue of his first name. "What can you tell me about him?"

Before Dr. Maharaj could answer, another giggle echoed down the hallway. "Girls," Dr. Maharaj said as he turned toward the candy stripers, a trace of a smile on his lips, "please report to Nurse Chaykowski. I'm sure she has plenty for you to do."

"Yes, Doctor Maharaj," the brunette candy striper said, her face reddening slightly as she and her blond companion looked through the patient's window one more time before they hurried down the hall.

"I apologize, Staff Sergeant Romanowski," Dr. Maharaj said. "They've been like that ever since he arrived."

"No problem. And call me Richard. I insist."

"Yes, of course. Please feel free to use my first name as well."

As Dr. Maharaj waited expectantly, Romanowski's heart rate shot up. Was this some kind of test? Why had he made that stupid first name comment in the first place? He swallowed hard. "You got it . . . Bash?" He winced slightly as he said it, almost certain he had gotten it wrong.

Dr. Maharaj smiled. "You nailed it—this time. Anyway, as for our patient . . ."

"Yes, what can you tell me about him? Still claiming he can't remember anything?"

Dr. Maharaj nodded. "Yes, but as I told you on the phone, it doesn't make any sense. He's suffered a nasty concussion, but that typically creates anterograde amnesia—an inability to create new memories after the traumatic event. But he's claiming to have retrograde amnesia, an inability to remember anything before the accident. He claims he doesn't remember where he was going, where he came from—"

"Or why the license plates on his car are supposed to be on a gold VW Rabbit in Regina instead of his navy-blue Plymouth Fury station wagon?"

"Exactly."

"What about the candy stripers?" Romanowski asked, nodding at them as they reappeared in the hall, grim-faced now as they pushed a cart loaded with adult diapers, wipes, and change pads toward a set of double doors labeled "Seniors' Ward."

"Well, apart from his scrapes and bruises, even I have to admit he's a handsome young man," Dr. Maharaj said. "It's all we can do to keep the girls away from him."

"Hmph," Romanowski replied. "Well, is it OK with you if I ask him a few questions?"

"Yes, of course," Dr. Maharaj said, leading the way toward the patient's room. "Be my guest."

§

Matt, Chad, Andrew, and Dean entered school together that morning, Matt still trying to pitch the other boys on his idea of building a monumental snow maze.

"Think about it, guys," he said. "People build corn

mazes all the time. The only thing that's different about this is it'll be tunnels instead of pathways through some boring farmer's field, and it'll be made out of snow instead of corn. That means you can't cheat like you can in a corn maze by just cutting through it to the next row."

"Not to mention the fact it could collapse at any moment, smothering our customers," Dean said.

"At least those people won't bother us for a refund," Chad joked.

"We can make it safe," Matt insisted, elbowing his brother to keep quiet. "We'll make sure the roof is thin, and we'll even build in escape hatches."

"How?" Chad inquired.

"I don't know," Matt said, pausing as his mind groped for an idea. "With plywood."

"Won't that ruin the snowy effect?" Dean asked.

"I don't know . . . we'll paint them white," Matt said. "And we'll have them every ten feet or so, so people are never far from one."

"That's actually not a bad idea," Andrew admitted. "We'll need a way to get snow out of some of the longer tunnels anyway, so your escape hatch idea kills two birds with one stone. It'll be difficult to tell the hatches apart from the snow, especially if we have people go through the maze at night."

"At night? That's a great idea," Matt said. Then he stopped and stared at his curly haired friend. "Wait a second, you mean you're actually considering this idea?"

Andrew held up his hands to temper Matt's enthusiasm. "Well, I didn't say—"

"Happy Valentine's Day!" a female voice said. They all looked up to see a girl named Joy approaching. She was relatively new to the school. Her family had moved to Milligan Creek just after Christmas, her father having taken over the town's dental clinic. Despite having only been in town for a few weeks, she had quickly established herself as a force to be reckoned with, getting herself nominated to serve on all sorts of committees, including the school's social committee. Despite the flurry of activity that she stirred up wherever she went, Joy always seemed to have time for one student in particular . . .

"Hello, Dean," she said, smiling sweetly.

"Did she just flutter her eyelashes?" Chad whispered.

Matt nodded, staring at Joy. "I think so."

"What do you mean?" Dean grumbled, barely able to bring himself to look at her. "Valentine's Day isn't until next week."

"I know," Joy said. "But it's never too early to start thinking about who you're going to ask to the big dance." She handed him a flyer that promoted the event. Dean held it as far away as possible as he read it, as if the paper were infected with a disease.

"Cupid is as Cupid Does? What kind of a name for a dance is that?"

Joy smiled even wider, if that were possible. "I don't know, Dean. After all, love is a mystery, as they say. I guess you'll just have to show up and find out."

"Fat chance," Dean said, about to crumple up the flyer.

"Wait! There's going to be a snow sculpture contest too," Joy said, putting her hand on his and turning the flyer over, so he could see the other side. He nearly jumped out of his skin at her touch. Then she stepped back and put one hand on her hip and the other under her chin as she struck a pose. "Let me know if you need a model."

"Good grief," Dean said, tilting his head back and closing his eyes in consternation.

"Ta-ta, boys," she said as she sashayed down the hall, seemingly energized by Dean's lack of enthusiasm.

"See ya later, Joy," Matt said, chuckling at Dean's melodramatics.

"Man, she really has the hots for you," Chad said once she was gone.

Dean let out a huff of air. "Tell me about it. She won't leave me alone."

"Well, now you know how Joyce has felt all these years," Matt pointed out.

"That's different," Dean said.

"Oh yeah? How?"

"Well, for starters, she's—"

Before Dean could continue, Joyce herself rounded the corner with a group of friends. Dean's mouth fell open as he watched her pass, though she was completely oblivious of him as she talked and laughed with the other girls.

Matt nudged Dean. "Stop staring!"

Dean shook his head as if he'd just been woken from a dream. "What? Oh. As I was saying . . ." Just then, he looked down at the flyer, then up at Joyce's retreating form, and his face broke into a huge grin. "I just got a terrific idea."

"Oh no you don't," Matt said. "There's no way you're asking Joyce to the dance."

Dean grinned as he hurried off down the hall. "Just you wait and see!"

Matt gave his brother a disgusted look. "Are you just going to stand there? Help me stop him!" He ran after Dean. Chad followed reluctantly, Andrew right behind them.

"Slow down!" Mr. Karky, their gym teacher, ordered as he swept by on his way to the gym wearing a black-and-white striped referee's uniform, a whistle dangling around his neck.

"Yes, Mr. Karky," the boys said, slowing to a fast walk. As soon as Mr. Karky was out of sight, they booked it after Dean.

§

Dewey was starting to think he could get used to hospital life. He had a comfortable bed, three meals a day, nurses and candy stripers waiting on him hand and foot, his own TV—it was like staying in a motel. That is, if motels required their guests to wear a gown that didn't quite close all the way in the back, the food looked like it had been molded out of plastic and tasted as if it had been warmed up over someone's truck engine, and the TV got only two fuzzy channels. But considering the motels that Dewey had stayed in over the years, his comparison wasn't too far off.

The only downside was his head. It hurt. Badly. That and the pesky doctor who kept coming in and asking him all those questions. Or were there two doctors? Sometimes Dewey could have sworn he was seeing double. But he was too afraid to ask for fear of learning just how bad his head injury really was. At any rate, the doctor—or doctors—didn't seem to believe a word Dewey said. Not that they should have, seeing as Dewey was merely pretending to have amnesia, but he'd always considered himself a pretty good liar, so he didn't know why his performance wasn't working. He claimed he couldn't remember where he was from, why he had been driving that night, or why his license plates didn't match his vehicle. All of that was a lie, but as a result of his concussion, there was one important piece of information he really couldn't remember—what had happened to the black hard-shell case. Was it still in the station wagon? If so, had the police officers who investigated the accident found it?

The moment that thought hit him, a jolt of fear shot through his insides. If he didn't figure out where the case was soon, he didn't even want to consider what the police would do if they figured out what was inside it—or what Earl would do if he found out Dewey had bungled the job.

Just as his imagination was starting to get the better of him, the door to his hospital room opened. Dewey jerked with a start, afraid it might actually be his boss. Instead, the first thing he saw was a mustache, followed by a badge . . . and a gun.

5

The Interrogation

Dewey swallowed hard. "G-good morning, Officer," he said as Staff Sergeant Romanowski entered his room.

"Good morning. Mr. Biggs, right?" Romanowski asked, consulting his notebook as the door swung shut behind him. "First name . . ."

"Dewey."

"Oh, so you do remember some things," Romanowski replied, looking up from his notes.

Dewey smiled weakly. "A few things, yes. The rest . . ." He shook his bandaged head and then winced at the pain and dizziness that the movement caused. "Kind of fuzzy."

"Mind taking off your sunglasses?" Romanowski asked. Dewey had been forced to wear sunglasses due to his concussion, which made him incredibly sensitive to light. He did as the officer asked, squinting and blinking as Romanowski compared Dewey's face to the one he had on file. "Okay, you can put them back on now."

"Thanks," Dewey said, feeling instant relief when he did. But even the sunglasses weren't enough. The next time he saw his nurse, he'd have to ask her for a hat to shield more of the light.

"So, you hit a moose," Romanowski said.

Dewey attempted another smile. "That's what they tell me."

The police officer eyed him skeptically. "You don't remember?"

Dewey shook his head—gently this time. "All I remember is a flash of white and then, whoosh, I woke up here."

"What's the last thing you remember before that?"

Dewey shrugged, thankful he was wearing sunglasses, so Romanowski couldn't see his eyes darting around the room as his mind raced to come up with a plausible answer.

"Do you remember where you bought that station wagon?" Romanowski asked.

"No."

"How about where you were going?"

"No."

"How about those license plates? Do you remember how they got onto your car?"

Dewey's heart rate spiked at that question. He was thankful he wasn't hooked up to a lie detector. "No."

"But you do remember that driving without insurance carries a penalty of up to five thousand dollars and/or imprisonment for up to five years, correct?"

"Yes," Dewey said, the mention of prison time momentarily causing him to forget his charade. "I mean no! That is, why would you bring that up?"

"The license plates on your car aren't yours. They came from another vehicle. The fine for stealing license plates is another five hundred dollars. How's your bank account looking, Mr. Biggs?"

"Not too bad—I mean, I don't remember."

"Uh-huh," Romanowski said, jotting down some

notes. "How about the time you spent in prison? Have any good memories from there?"

Dewey shook his head, slowly. At least he wasn't lying about that.

Romanowski made another notation in his notebook, his mustache wriggling as he scribbled. Dewey leaned forward slightly, trying to catch a glimpse at what he was writing. When Romanowski snapped his notebook shut, Dewey quickly leaned back again, unable to read the police officer's scrawl.

"Well, I'm not going to charge you with anything yet," Romanowski said. "I need to do a bit more investigating first. But I'm advising you not to leave town. If you do, you will be charged with fleeing a police officer, which can result in a thousand-dollar fine and up to three years in prison on top of all the other potential charges. Is that clear?"

Dewey swallowed hard. "Yes, Officer."

Romanowski dug into the pocket of his RCMP-issue parka. "Here's my card," he said, handing it to Dewey. "In case anything comes back to you, give me a call."

"Yes, sir," Dewey said, looking at the card. "Romanowski," he said, reading it aloud. "My seventh-grade teacher was a Romanowski."

"Oh yeah?" the staff sergeant said, pausing at the door. "Where'd you grow up?"

Dewey was about to answer but then he shrugged, realizing he shouldn't be able to recall that either. Romanowski offered a skeptical smile. "Let me guess, you don't remember."

Dewey shook his head. Romanowski heaved out a deep breath. "Look, Mr. Biggs—Dewey. You're facing some serious charges here. If you're doing this whole 'I can't remember' thing to protect someone or because you're afraid of someone else finding out you talked to the police, we can help you. All we need is your cooperation. Even if you've done something wrong, the courts will go easier on you if you provide some assistance."

"Thank you, Officer," Dewey said, holding up the card. "The minute anything comes back to me, you'll be the first person I call."

Romanowski nodded, not believing a word of it. "Just don't leave town."

Dewey smiled and gestured to his room. "And lose all this? Not a chance."

Romanowski sniffed in amusement. "Enjoy it while you can, Mr. Biggs."

§

Matt, Chad, and Andrew finally caught up with Dean just outside the school office.

"What the heck are you doing?" Matt asked, huffing from exertion.

"Anyone got a pen?" Dean asked, ignoring Matt's question.

"Here," Andrew said, pulling one out of his binder and handing it to him.

"You're seriously helping him?" Matt asked, looking at Andrew in disgust.

Andrew shrugged. "It's just a pen."

"And it's just a snow sculpture contest," Chad pointed out as Dean scrawled his name on a sign-up sheet taped to the white cinder-block wall.

"Oh yeah? What—or who—are you going to sculpt?" Matt asked, eyeing Dean suspiciously.

"You'll see soon enough," Dean said, a smile plastered

across his face. "Thanks for the pen," he added, tossing it back to Andrew. "Now if you'll excuse me, I don't want to be late for class."

"What do you suppose he's up to?" Matt asked as he watched Dean walk jauntily down the hall, whistling to himself.

"No idea," Chad said as the bell rang. "But like Joy said, I guess you'll have to show up at the dance and find out."

"What about the snow maze?" Matt asked as he followed the other boys toward class.

"Let's meet in the tree house and talk about it after school," Andrew said.

§

As soon as Romanowski left his hospital room, Dewey tossed the business card onto his bedside table and then lay back on his pillows in relief. Despite a few slip-ups, he thought he had performed rather well. He knew Romanowski probably didn't believe a word he had said, but the small-town cop couldn't prove anything beyond the stolen license plates. And despite Romanowski's threats of incarceration, no one went to prison for such things in Saskatchewan—at least Dewey hoped not. So, the worst he was looking at was a few hundred dollars in fines and possibly a suspension of his driver's license. But he'd lived without a license before; he'd just take the bus. As for the fines, good luck getting that from his non-existent savings account.

While the legal issues caused him some stress, he was more concerned about the one thing he truly couldn't remember—the location of the hard-shell case. The fact Romanowski hadn't brought it up meant the police probably hadn't found it in the station wagon—unless he was trying to trick Dewey somehow.

Curiously, the padlock Dewey always wore around his neck was also gone, although the chain was still around his neck. He had asked the nurses about the padlock, but no one had seen it, though the key had been found in his pants pocket.

What worried Dewey most was breaking the news to Earl. The plan had been for Dewey to call him as soon as he reached Saskatoon. The snowstorm had probably bought him a bit of time, but if he didn't call soon, Earl would become suspicious that Dewey had run off with the case or gone to the police. But if Dewey did call Earl, what would he tell him? That he had lost the most valuable prize that Earl had ever sent him to recover? What then? He'd never known Earl to be violent—at least not to him. But Earl was big, and he had a temper, and there was always a first time. And if not Earl, there was always his right-hand man, Clive . . .

Some giggling at the window drew Dewey's attention. He looked up and saw the two candy stripers peeking through his window. He smiled and waved, eliciting a second round of giggles before Nurse Chaykowski yelled at the girls to get back to work, and they quickly disappeared. Seconds later, Nurse Chaykowski's glowering face appeared at the window. He waved at her as well, but she just scowled and walked away.

The excitement over, Dewey settled back into his pillows, suddenly feeling sleepy—probably a side effect of his concussion and the meds they had given him. Despite his worries about Earl and the police, it was nice to rest. Besides, he was pretty certain Earl had no idea where he was. So, for the moment at least, he could rest in peace . . .

6

Location Scouts

"Bad news, guys," Andrew said as he flipped open the trapdoor in the floor of the tree house, which was located in the shelter belt that surrounded Matt and Chad's acreage. Matt, Chad, and Dean were already sitting around the table inside the reclaimed MD 500 Defender helicopter fuselage, complete with round bubble windshield, which formed the central part of the tree house. The rest of the structure was made from more traditional materials, including a hodgepodge of salvaged wood, windows taken from an old shop that the Taylors had torn down, and a corrugated metal roof, salvaged from that same shop. It was an ongoing construction project, the boys constantly adding new features, including bunk beds, bookshelves, shutters, and window boxes full of flowers. The previous summer, they had also added the cab from an old Gleaner combine, which doubled as a sunroom and a greenhouse. The tree house also had electricity, thanks to an extension cord that ran to a power pole in the yard. It was currently powering a small space heater, which kept the structure relatively toasty despite the cool winter weather.

"What's the matter?" Matt asked. "Did your subscription to Popular Science just run out?" He grinned at the others, who couldn't help but chuckle. Andrew was a true science geek, obsessed with everything from astronomy to quantum physics. Although his scientific and engineering knowledge often came in handy during the boys' numerous adventures, they never passed up a chance to rib him about it.

"No," Andrew said. "In fact, the latest issue just arrived, and the cover story is on Apple's new thirty-two-bit mini Mac, which I can't wait to read about. But never mind that. I'm talking about the snow maze. Before I came over, I called the owner of the field that Dean landed in after his jump, and he won't give us permission to build the snow maze there. He said it sounds like fun, but he doesn't want to be on the hook in case someone gets hurt."

Dean looked around at the others. "Did I miss something? Are we actually going ahead with this?"

Matt sank back into his bucket seat. "We were until Andrew showed up—which you'd know if you weren't so fixated on asking Joyce to go with you to the Valentine's Day dance."

"Who said I was asking Joyce to the dance?" Dean said. "All I did was enter the snow sculpture contest."

"Yeah, well, there's still something fishy about it," Matt replied. "Since when have you ever sculpted anything?"

Dean was about to respond when Chad stepped in. "So that's it then?" he asked Andrew. "The maze idea is out?"

"Not necessarily," Andrew said, pulling a long cardboard tube out of his backpack. He opened one end of it and pulled out a laminated map, which he spread on the table in front of the other boys. They quickly set coffee mugs, magazines, and other items on each corner, so it would lay flat. The map showed all the agricultural land around the town of Milligan Creek as well as who owned it. "I was looking at this map after school," Andrew said, "and it made me wonder if some other locations might work just as well. After all, that gully is quite a distance from town and impossible to access from the road. We'd have to bring people to and from the maze on snowmobiles, which would be tedious, not to mention expensive in terms of fuel."

Matt scrutinized the map, as did the other boys. "I'm not sure I understand," he said. "This map tells us who owns all the land around Milligan Creek, which is great, but how do we know where other huge snow deposits might have formed, like in that gully?"

"Using these," Andrew said, pointing at the curved lines that undulated across the map. "These are contour lines. They indicate the elevation of each area. Snowdrifts form on the lee or downwind side of trees, buildings, or hills that slow the wind enough to cause it to drop some of the snow it's carrying. For example, those trees along the west side of the gully where Dean got stuck were probably the main reason why there was so much snow there. They slowed down the wind, making the snow too heavy for the wind to carry, and it dropped it all in the gully. Seeing as the prevailing wind typically comes from the west, all we need to do is find a spot near a road close to town that has a high elevation on the west side. Someplace with a creek or a gully and some trees would be ideal. Then we can ask the landowner for permission to tunnel there."

"Well, what are we waiting for?" Matt asked, already running his index finger over the map as he searched for potential spots. "Let's get started!"

§

In his hospital room, Dewey awoke with a start. He looked around, terrified of who he might discover—Earl or that pesky police officer or even worse, Earl's right-hand man, Clive—but he was all alone. Not even the candy stripers were hanging around outside his window. He pressed the button that made the upper half of his bed tilt forward, so he was sitting rather than lying down. He stopped suddenly as a series of images from his recent dream flashed through his brain: barbed wire, blowing snow, a gravel road . . . and a padlock. His padlock!

His hand went automatically to the chain around his neck. What did his padlock have to do with a barbed-wire fence? Could it be connected with the hard-shell case? Of course! More pieces of that fateful evening came flooding back to him. The snowstorm, the flashing red-and-blue lights, the gravel road, the moose, the snow scraper . . . the gravel road! That was it! He had buried the case in the snow along a gravel road and marked the spot on a barbed-wire fence with his padlock.

He was so excited that he practically leaped out of bed, then fell back onto his pillows, his head pounding. After waiting for the top of his skull to stop throbbing and his vision to clear, he stood shakily to his feet and hobbled over to the closet in the corner, taking out the clear plastic bag that contained his clothes and other personal items. As restful and relaxing as his stay in the hospital had been, Dewey knew it was only a matter of time before Earl figured out where he was, if he hadn't already, and there was no way Dewey wanted Earl to show up until he had found that case. Concussion or not, Dewey had no choice but to look for it—or die trying.

§

Earl Jones slammed his phone down and sat back in his creaky leather office chair, which was situated behind a large double-pedestal oak desk in a wood-paneled office that was saturated with years of stale cigarette smoke. The light cast by the green-shaded banker's lamp on the big man's desk gave his skin an eerie glow and created menacing shadows on his craggy, unshaven face. He sat there in silence, running his hand through his thick, wavy, salt-and-pepper hair as he stared at the map of Saskatchewan laid across his desk. Then he pounded his fist in frustration. "For the love of Pete! Where is that stupid kid?"

His outburst was interrupted by a gentle knock on his door.

"Whaddaya want?" Earl said, not looking up. His eyes remained fixed on the map, focusing in particular on the Yellowhead Highway between Winnipeg and Saskatoon, the latter of which was where his office was located. It was situated in an auto-wrecking yard that was no longer in business, though the building was still surrounded by an acre of rusting, discarded automobiles and other junk, the perfect cover for his clandestine activities.

"I have your morning tea, sir." His assistant, Clive, pushed the door open with his back as he entered the room bearing a silver tray. On it was a teapot, a teacup and saucer, and a plate of English shortbread. Earl realized his affinity for tea and fine china didn't exactly enhance his tough-guy image, but he also knew his employees and associates were too intimidated by him to rib him about it. His love for tea was a carryover from being raised by his Cockney grandmother, God rest her soul. Besides, it comforted him during times of trouble, and it helped him think.

"Just put it on the desk," Earl grumbled.

"As you wish, sir."

Like Earl's grandmother, Clive was also a British import, having emigrated to Canada from a rough part of Birmingham, England, when he was thirteen years old. His parents had hoped that sending him to live with relatives in Regina would break his affinity for break-and-enters, vandalism, graffiti, and other petty crimes. However, if anything, being forced to leave his friends and move to another country only increased Clive's appetite for destruction. It didn't take long for him to run afoul of the justice system in Canada, just as he had back home, which was how he and Earl met.

As bunkmates in a prison camp in northern Saskatchewan, Earl had taken a liking to the young Brit almost immediately—due in no small part to Clive's accent, which reminded him of his grandmother—and he became Clive's de facto protector. In return, Clive ran small errands for Earl at the camp, a role he continued after they were released. Over time, Clive became Earl's most trusted confidante and advisor—and occasional hatchet man. Compared to Earl, Clive didn't look dangerous, but every once in a while, if the lighting was just right, a glimmer of suppressed anger could be seen simmering just below the surface of his eyes, waiting to be unleashed.

"Problems, sir?" Clive inquired, acting every bit the Alfred to Earl's Bruce Wayne as he poured a cup of tea for his boss.

"Knock it off with that butler schtick," Earl said, grabbing his teacup and taking a slurp. "You know as well as I do what's gotten me so hot and bothered. It's that numbskull, Dewey. He was supposed to report back to me as soon as he made it to Saskatoon, but it's been over a day now, and I haven't heard a peep. Neither has anyone else. It's like the stupid kid just disappeared." He grabbed a shortbread cookie and tossed it into his mouth, munching it fiercely. "How does anyone disappear in a place as flat as Saskatchewan?"

"If you don't mind my saying, sir, I knew the mission might have been a bit too much for him."

Earl glared at Clive as he finished chewing his cookie and then swallowed. "You saying I made a mistake?"

"Of course not, sir," Clive replied, wiping a few stray wet crumbs off his shirt that had spewed out of Earl's mouth. "Only that you tend to overestimate people's capabilities—and their loyalty."

Earl took another gulp of tea to wash down the cookie and refilled his cup as he pondered Clive's words. "You telling me you think Dewey's run off with the case? You think he might have taken it to someone else?"

Clive shrugged. "For all we know, he may have taken it to the police. He could have gotten cold feet and be 'spilling the beans,' as they say, right now."

Earl considered the possibility, then shook his head. "Naw, not Dewey. He may be a numbskull, and he may be incompetent, but he's no rat." He turned back to the map. "Something else is going on here. I just can't figure out what."

"Perhaps you should send someone else to look for him, retrace his steps," Clive suggested. Earl sat back in his chair and grabbed another piece of shortbread, chewing it thoughtfully.

"Oh yeah?" he said. "And who do you suggest?"

"You know I love a good road trip, sir."

Earl's eyebrows shot up in surprise. "You? You get carsick on the way between here and Robin's Donuts, and it's only three blocks away!"

"Not if I'm driving," Clive pointed out.

"Hmph," Earl replied, still chewing. "I don't know. I need you around here, Clive."

Clive took a deep breath. "Not to denigrate my very important duties here, sir, but there's nothing I do for you on a day-to-day basis that I can't train one of your monkeys to do in my place."

"I don't know—wait a second, did you just call my people monkeys?"

Clive shrugged. "Highly trained monkeys, sir."

Earl thought about it and then grunted, letting it pass. Good help was hard to find, after all. "As I was saying, I'm not sure if I can do without you, Clive. It's not just the errands and other duties you perform for me. You're the only person in my organization who I trust. And you make a heckuva cup of tea." Earl held his cup out to emphasize his point before taking another sip.

"Which is exactly why you should send me on this mission," Clive said, refilling Earl's cup as soon as he set it back on the tray.

Earl frowned in confusion. "Because of the tea?"

"No, because of another kind of tea. Loyalty." Clive replied. "You've already had one man go missing with that case. Who's to say if you send someone else, he won't go missing too?"

Earl hated to admit it, but Clive was right. Not only were most of his employees nincompoops, he didn't trust them for a second. Clive, on the other hand . . .

"Okay," Earl said, pushing his tea service aside and picking up the map, folding it as he talked. "I'll give you one week. Retrace Dewey's route, starting here and working your way back to Winnipeg. Leave no stone unturned.

Stop in every town along the way, big and small, and find out if anybody's seen him. You'll need this . . ." He handed Clive the map. "And these." He opened his top desk drawer and pulled out a set of car keys, tossing them to Clive.

"Won't I be needing something else, sir?" Clive asked, holding out his right hand and rubbing his thumb, index, and middle fingers together.

"Oh, right," Earl said. "Just one minute." Clive turned his back on the big man as Earl spun around in his chair and turned the dial on the huge safe that sat behind his desk. After wrenching it open, Earl withdrew a wad of cash, slammed the safe door, and then plunked the money onto his desk.

"Don't spend it all in one place," he warned. "And two-star motels only," he added as Clive pocketed the cash. "None of those luxury suites I know you love so much."

"Of course, sir. And please, put your fears to rest. You can count on me."

"Hmph," Earl said, settling back into his chair as he grabbed another piece of shortbread. "We'll see about that. Just don't come back until you've found Dewey—and that case."

7

The Search Begins

After pinpointing several potential locations for the snow maze on Andrew's map, the boys set out to scout them. Wanting to keep the project a secret at least until they had a solid game plan, rather than get one of their parents to drive them around to the various spots, they decided to travel by snowmobile. Matt and Chad rode on their sled, and Dean rode behind Andrew on his machine. They cut across fields and zoomed through ditches, those on the back of the snow machines struggling to hold on over all the bumps.

"Could you at least slow it down over the bigger drifts?" Dean pleaded.

"Sorry," Andrew called back over his shoulder as he eased back on the throttle. "We're almost there."

A couple of minutes later, he brought the snowmobile to a stop, Chad and Matt zooming up beside them. "That took longer than I thought it would," Matt said, shutting down the machine and hopping off, a pleasant whiff of two-stroke engine exhaust filling the brisk winter air.

"Tell me about it," Chad said, easing himself off the rear seat. "We hit so many bumps, I don't think I'll be able to straighten out my back for a week."

"Well, how does it look?" Matt asked, eager to nail down a location as soon as possible, so they could start digging—and advertising. Their first choice was a site along the gully carved out by Milligan Creek itself, which seemed fitting considering some of their earlier adventures.

"At first glance, not as good as I thought it would be," Andrew said. They were just downstream from the dam, which was located south of town. As indicated by the contour lines on the map, the land fell away nicely on the westward side, but whoever owned it had recently knocked down a stand of bush along the edge of the gully, which would have made an ideal windbreak. Snowdrifts had formed around the piles of trees that had been left behind, but none of them extended into the gully itself.

"That's too bad," Chad said. "I was really rooting for this spot. I even came up with the perfect tagline: 'Best snow maze in the world by a dam site!'"

Dean flashed him a concerned look. "Wait a second, did you just say—oh, I get it," he said, smiling as he pointed at the dam. "You meant D-A-M, not D-A-M—"

"It doesn't matter what he meant," Matt said, already heading back toward the snowmobiles. "This spot isn't going to work. Let's keep moving."

With a final longing look at the gully, the other boys hurried after him.

§

Despite the doctor's protests—Dewey still wasn't sure if there were two doctors who looked exactly the same or if he was just seeing double—not to mention the nurses (and the candy stripers, who were in tears), Dewey checked himself out of the hospital. Though still a bit shaky on his feet, he insisted he was well enough to leave on his own. With the help of his sunglasses, a rumpled cap advertising a local welding business that he had commandeered from the hospital's lost-and-found, and an umbrella that he had swiped from a stand just inside the front door, he strode confidently into the crisp, clear February day—then stopped short, doubling over in pain.

"My eyes! My eyes!" he cried, squeezing them shut to block out the sunlight, which was doubly blinding as it reflected off the snow all around him.

"Is everything OK, Mr. Biggs?" Dr. Maharaj asked as he poked his head out the hospital's front doors, shivering in his lab coat. "You sure you don't want to reconsider?"

"Yeah, it's freezing out here," the other Dr. Maharaj said as he joined his brother at the door. Dewey stared at them in confusion, then gently shook his head to clear his vision, but when he looked again, he was still seeing double. Or was he?

"No, I'm fine," Dewey said, still bent over. He waved awkwardly, then straightened up somewhat and began walking. He found that if he pulled the cap low over his eyes, squinted, and held the umbrella just right, he could barely tolerate the sunlight penetrating his eyes, though seeing where he was going was a different matter altogether.

Harpreet shook his head. "Some people have to learn things the hard way, I guess," he said as he and Bash watched Dewey hobble down the street.

Bash turned to his brother. "You mean it's not just you?"

Harpreet grinned. "Do I have to remind you again which one of us was named the valedictorian of our medical school, and which one received the award for Most Improved Scalpel Sharpener?"

"You know that's only because they couldn't tell the two of us apart," Bash said as he followed Harpreet back inside. "Besides, what about that time right after we arrived in Canada when you nearly performed an appendectomy on the wrong patient?"

"How was I supposed to know that 'Billy' could be a girl's name too?" Harpreet asked.

The brothers were so caught up in their good-natured ribbing that they forgot all about Dewey. Had they looked back, they would have been just in time to see him step to the side to avoid a pile of doggy doo that someone had left in the middle of the sidewalk, lose his balance due to dizziness and nausea, and topple over into the snowbank.

§

As the boys drew near to their second location, they eased back on the throttles and glided to a stop.

"Road closed?" Matt said, standing up on the snowmobile and raising the face shield on his helmet, so he could see past the orange barricade that was blocking the road. "Who closes a road in the middle of winter? And what's wrong with it? It looks perfectly fine to me."

Just then, Andrew smacked himself in the helmet. "Sorry, guys, I totally forgot. My dad told me they took the bridge out a couple of weeks ago about half a mile past this barricade."

"So they'll probably put a new one in soon, right?" Matt said.

Andrew shook his head. "No. That's why my dad was talking about it. They're not going to replace it until spring.

Something to do with a labor dispute with the contractor who's supposed to install it. Anyway, the farmers around here are ticked because now they have to take the long way around to get to town."

"Well, they aren't the only ones who are ticked," Matt said, slamming his face shield back down and starting his snowmobile. "We can forget about this location. Nobody would be able to drive to it. Let's keep moving."

§

The bell above the door to the Co-op Hardware Store dinged, setting off a chorus of barking and snorting as two energetic pugs raced out from under the counter to investigate.

"Don't mind Cliff and Benji," the clerk, Max Olafson, a portly man in his early sixties, said as he made a notation in a ledger beside the cash register. "They're just curious—" He stopped short when he looked up over his reading glasses to see who had come in. His eyes were met by a strange apparition—a man wearing sunglasses and a rumpled ball cap and carrying . . . an umbrella? In February?

"Can I help you, sir?" Max asked, setting his pen down as the pugs wound in and around Dewey's legs, sniffing him as if he'd just spent the last ten minutes rolling around in a barrel full of sausages.

"Yes," Dewey said, about to close the umbrella and then thinking better of it when the bright fluorescent lights hit his eyes.

"Cliff, Benji, leave him alone!" Max said, straightening up and hooking his thumbs through his suspenders (he'd given up on belts years ago due to his protruding belly). With a final sniff, the dogs turned and waddled back toward Max, disappearing behind the counter. "What can I do for you, Mr. . . ."

"I'd like a shovel," Dewey said. "Can you point me toward them?"

Thumbs still hooked in his suspenders, Max smiled. "I certainly can. They're right beside you. What kind of shovel are you looking for?" Dewey turned to examine the display. A variety of shovels were leaning against the front window. "We've got snow shovels, sleigh shovels, rink shovels, trunk shovels, plastic shovels, metal shovels, ice scrapers, you name it."

Dewey bent over and picked up a small shovel with a retractable handle that slid forward into the blade, making it lightweight and compact. "How much is this one?"

"That little fella? It may not look like much, but it's got an aluminum blade, an ergonomic design, and that telescopic handle expands an extra twenty inches. All you gotta do is give it a twist and a pull and—bam! You're ready to move some serious snow."

"And the price?" Dewey asked, growing impatient with the unsolicited sales pitch, which Max thought was necessary to justify the shovel's price.

"Only twenty-nine ninety-nine," Max said, cringing as he said it. "I know it sounds expensive, but—"

"I'll take it," Dewey said, approaching the cash register. "I'll take one of those Maglites too." He pointed to where they hung behind the counter. "And some batteries." As he set the shovel on the counter and dug in his pocket for his wallet, Max grabbed a Maglite and some batteries and then turned back and looked Dewey up and down.

"So, going to do some digging, are you?"

Rather than respond, Dewey held out his umbrella. "Do you mind holding this?"

"Certainly." Max took it from Dewey, so he had both hands free to extract some rumpled bills from his wallet. Max looked up at the umbrella. "There some rain in the forecast that I don't know about? I know it's only February, but stranger things have happened . . ." His voice trailed off as Dewey looked around and sniffed, then put his fist to his mouth to stifle his gag reflex.

"That smell, what's—" He paused to stifle another gag. Max watched him, mystified, and then his eyes lit up.

"Oh, that! That's just the boys." Max pointed under the counter, where the dogs were snuffling around. "Knock it off!" Max said, looking down at them and then turning back to Dewey. "Flatulent little critters. It's the breed. The way I see it, their noses are pressed so flat, they have a hard time getting air out the front end, so the only place left for it to go is—"

"Keep the change," Dewey said, plunking his money on the counter. Eager to get away from the smell, he shoved the Maglite and batteries in his coat pockets, grabbed the shovel, and took his umbrella back from Max.

"Oh, uh, thanks," Max said, unaccustomed to such abruptness. "Nice doing business with you!" Dewey waved the shovel in reply, not looking back. The second the bell above the door dinged, the dogs came ripping out from behind the counter, emitting another explosion of barking and snorting. "Cliff, Benji, knock it off!" Max yelled.

§

Having spent the entire afternoon scouting various locations for the snow maze but still coming up empty, the boys climbed the ladder into the tree house, then plunked down in the bucket seats around the central table, exhausted and disappointed by their fruitless search. Whether due to roadblocks, trees being knocked down, or livestock being in the way, each potential location had proved unworkable for one reason or another.

"Maybe we need to expand our search a bit farther from town," Matt said. He turned to Andrew. "Mind pulling out your map?" Andrew grabbed the tube and handed it to Matt, who pulled out the map and then unrolled it across the table. "As I was saying, I think we need to look farther afield. I mean, if people will travel one mile to get to the snow maze, they'll travel two miles."

"Uh, we don't know if anyone will travel at all to go through our maze," Dean said. "I don't even know if I will. I can already hear what my mother will say when she hears about it."

"You haven't told her, have you?" Matt asked, eyeing him suspiciously, as did the other boys.

"No!" Dean insisted, his eyes meeting their accusing glares. As they'd learned all too well during their recent water war and other adventures, Dean's mother was a force to be reckoned with. The last thing any of them wanted was her shutting down the snow maze before they'd even begun digging, which is exactly what she'd do, especially if she discovered it was Matt's idea.

"OK then," Matt said, turning back to the map. "Let's see if we can find some new spots."

§

Clive hadn't been completely honest with Earl when he had asked his permission to go looking for Dewey, but he had told the truth about one thing: he loved a good road trip. With his hands at "ten and two" on the steering wheel, Clive smiled and filled his lungs with the new car smell as he sped down the highway. Unlike Dewey, who had been forced to drive an old clunker, Earl had given Clive the keys to a brand-new Chrysler New Yorker. It had a state-of-the art digital speedometer, stereo, and clock. It also had electric windows, locks, and seats, and it even spoke! If Clive left the keys in the ignition when he opened the door, it said, "A door is ajar." He couldn't get enough of it.

Although Clive hadn't been completely truthful with Earl, he hadn't exactly lied to him either. He had merely withheld a crucial bit of information. What he didn't tell him was that this was the last mission he was going to do for the big man—ever! It wasn't that Earl was a bad boss, but Clive had played second fiddle to him long enough. He was ready to strike out on his own, and Earl had just unwittingly handed him everything he needed to do it. While Clive definitely wanted to find Dewey, he had no plans to return him or the hard-shell case to Earl once he did. Having recently discovered what was in the case, Clive planned to keep it for himself. As for Dewey, Clive's eyes glinted with malice at the thought of what he had in store for him. But first he had to get his hands on the disloyal little rat. He glanced at the blue lights of the digital clock on the dashboard and smiled. He was confident it was only a matter of time . . .

§

Dewey was cold—and miserable. Shuffling along the shoulder of the highway, umbrella in one hand and snow shovel in the other, he was a pitiful sight. Glancing nervously over his shoulder, he knew he was a conspicuous sight too. Considering Staff Sergeant Romanowski's warning not to leave town, he was taking a big chance walking down the highway in the open. But with his station wagon impounded, if not totaled from his collision with the moose, he had no choice. Besides, having waited until early evening before setting out, he hoped the chances of being spotted by the police—or Earl or Clive, God forbid—were close to nil.

When the sun dipped below the eastern horizon, Dewey instantly felt some relief, to the point he felt confident to lower his umbrella. A moment later, his eyes still smarting even in the sun's fading orange glow, he quickly popped it back up, then continued down the highway, shivering in the rapidly cooling evening air.

He really had no idea where he was going. Apart from the images of a gravel road and a barbed-wire fence that had flashed through his mind, he didn't have much to go on. But he had to start somewhere, and having seen a gravel road half a mile ahead, he figured he might as well start there. He zipped his coat right to the top and pulled his toque as far down over his ears as possible. It was going to be a long, cold night.

8

Sabotaged

The following morning was a Saturday. Thankful there was no school, the boys were looking forward to spending the entire day scouting for snow maze locations. That is, all the boys except Dean.

He was sitting at his kitchen table hunched over a bowl of Honeycomb cereal, shoveling it into his mouth as he watched an episode of the old 1967 Spider-Man cartoon series on TV, one of his favorite shows. Currently, Spider-Man was riding on top of a train carrying components for a top-secret military weapon. Just as his spidey sense started tingling, the train's headlights revealed a strange grey figure running down the tracks, heading straight for the train.

Right before the climactic moment, the phone rang. At first, Dean was too caught up in the action to notice it, never mind answer it.

"Deaaann!" his mother called from downstairs, where she was doing laundry. "Can you get that?"

"Get what?" Dean said through a mouthful of cereal, his eyes glued to the TV. Seconds later, the grey figure—a super-villain known as the Rhino—plowed into the train, obliterating it and sending Spider-Man flying into the wreckage.

"The phone!" Mrs. Muller yelled. The incessant ringing finally registering in his brain, Dean looked at the beige device, which hung on a wall in the kitchen.

"Why can't Dad get it?"

"Because he's out on a job! Now hurry before they hang up! It could be a client calling for him!"

Dean's dad was an electrician, and he often did emergency calls on the weekend. Considering his line of work, Mr. Muller should have had an answering machine, but he was also a bit on the cheap side, so if he missed a call, he missed a call. It had never occurred to him that if the answering machine saved him from missing just one potential job, it would more than pay for itself.

With a final glance at the TV—Spider-Man was fleeing the scene in case the authorities thought that he, not the Rhino, was the one who had stolen the weapons components—Dean picked up the phone.

"Hello?"

"Dean! Where are you?" Matt asked.

"What do you mean?" Dean said as the TV cut to a commercial for a Masters of the Universe slime pit playset. "I'm talking to you on the phone, so clearly I'm at home in my kitchen."

"No kidding," Matt said. "But why aren't you here?"

"Where?"

"The tree house!"

"You have a phone in the tree house now? Cool!"

"No! I meant our house. We're supposed to go out location scouting today, remember? Everyone else is here waiting for you."

"Seriously?" Dean asked, leaning forward in his chair,

so he could see the thermometer outside the window. It said it was -10°C outside. "Can't we wait until it warms up a little? Besides, I was going to spend the morning working on my snow sculpture."

"Your snow sculpture? Are you kidding me? Come on, Dean, we've a lot of ground to cover."

Just then, Dean heard his mother's feet thumping up the stairs. He watched as she entered the kitchen lugging a laundry basket piled high with clean clothes to be folded.

"Who's on the phone?" she whispered, peering around the mound of clothes.

Dean put his hand over the receiver, his mind racing for an answer. "Telemarketer," he replied.

"Tell him we're not interested!" she hissed, then headed into the living room, so she could fold the laundry while watching TV. Dean nodded and then removed his hand from the receiver.

"Uh, I'm sorry, sir, but our heating ducts have already been cleaned, and we don't need, uh, a carpet doctor—whatever that is."

"What the heck are you talking about?" Matt asked.

"Sorry," Dean replied. "Gotta go."

Back at Matt and Chad's house, Matt frowned at the receiver and then hung up.

"What's going on?" Chad asked, standing in the kitchen doorway in his snow gear, his snowmobile helmet tucked under one arm.

"I think Dean just ditched us," Matt said, turning to him. "He said he wanted to work on his snow sculpture instead."

Right then, Joyce sauntered into the kitchen in her nightgown, her face creased from sleep. She opened the fridge and perused its contents.

"Matt drank the last of the orange juice, if that's what you're looking for," Chad said.

She shrugged. "Grapefruit juice it is then." She took the container from the fridge and kicked the door shut with her foot. Matt eyed her with suspicion as she went to the cupboard to get a glass.

"Dean hasn't said anything to you recently, has he?"

Joyce scoffed. "Why would Dean say anything to me?" She poured herself a glass of grapefruit juice. "And why would I listen if he did?" She gave Matt a look as she passed him on her way back to the fridge, indicating he should know better.

Matt glanced at Andrew, who had joined Chad in the kitchen doorway. "Oh, no reason. By the way, you have a date for the Valentine's Day dance yet?"

She paused and looked at him, holding the fridge door open. "Why? Who wants to know?"

Matt reddened. "Uh, no one."

"Do you have a date for the dance?" Joyce asked.

Now it was Matt's turn to scoff. "No. Why would I want to go to a stupid thing like that?"

"Maybe because it's good to hang out with members of the opposite sex once in a while instead of getting into trouble with these clowns all the time."

"Yeah, well, there's plenty of time for that when we get older," Matt said, grabbing his snowmobile helmet off the kitchen table. He paused in the doorway. "If Dean does happen to say something to you—"

"Goodbye, boys," Joyce said, waving dismissively as she headed back to her room, a glass of grapefruit juice and a piece of bacon left over from the boys' breakfast in hand.

"Give it a rest," Chad said once she was gone. "Since

when have you been such a protective little brother?"

"Think about it," Matt said. "Dean's a good friend and all, but would you really want him as your brother-in-law?"

Chad grinned. "Good point. But fat chance of that happening."

"Speaking of Dean," Andrew said. "What should we do about scouting?"

"I guess we do it without him," Matt replied. "You snooze, you lose."

§

"He did what?" Staff Sergeant Romanowski exclaimed, both hands grasping the front desk of the Milligan Creek Hospital. Looking a bit rattled, Nurse Chaykowski, a few stray wisps of hair having escaped the bun at the back of her head and floating around her face, consulted her records once again.

"Dewey Biggs. Yes, he checked himself out yesterday afternoon."

Romanowski exhaled in disgust. "What is this place, a hotel?"

Nurse Chaykowski looked up at him over her glasses, having regained a measure of confidence in response to his brusque tone. "No, Staff Sergeant Romanowski, this is not a hotel, but neither is it a jail. Unlike the RCMP, we aren't in the habit of holding people against their will."

"I'm sorry, Sharon. I don't mean to be so gruff. It's just that—"

"Is there a problem, Officer?"

Romanowski turned to see Dr. Maharaj approaching, though he was too flustered and impatient to figure out if it was Bash or Harpreet. "Not this again," he muttered.

"Excuse me?" Dr. Maharaj said.

"Oh, nothing. It's just that . . . Dewey Biggs. You allowed him to discharge himself?"

Dr. Maharaj glanced at Nurse Chaykowski. "Were we under orders not to?"

"No, no, nothing like that," Romanowski said. "It's just that, as you know, we're still investigating the accident, and we have some suspicions regarding his vehicle. I warned him not to leave town. I guess I should have told you—or your brother. Anyway, do you have any idea where Mr. Biggs went?"

"Last seen hobbling toward downtown," Dr. Maharaj said. "I'm sorry we didn't think to consult you before we released him, but he was quite insistent, though my brother and I agreed he was in no shape to leave."

"Hmph," Romanowski replied as he pondered how to deal with this new development.

"While you're here," Dr. Maharaj said, "my wife and I have been wanting to have you over for dinner for some time now. Would you happen to be free next Tuesday evening?"

"Uh, yes," the staff sergeant said, his eyes raking the doctor's face for clues as to which Maharaj brother he was talking to.

"Splendid," Dr. Maharaj said. "Let's say six o'clock. Do you like curry, Staff Sergeant?"

"Yes. That is, as long as it's not too spicy." He patted his stomach. "Tends to give me bad dreams."

"Mild it is then. See you on Tuesday. You know where our house is, correct?"

"Yes, uh, of course."

"Good. We'll see you then." He turned away to resume his rounds.

"Just one second," Romanowski said.

Dr. Maharaj stopped and turned back, an inquisitive look on his face. "Yes?"

Romanowski was about to confirm the doctor's first name but then thought better of it. "Oh, uh, I was just wondering if I could bring anything."

Dr. Maharaj smiled, his white teeth glistening. "Only yourself—unless you'd like to bring a date, of course." For some reason, Dr. Maharaj's eyes leapt to Nurse Chaykowski. Romanowski glanced at her and did a double take as she batted her eyelashes at him. He quickly looked away. Was this some kind of a setup?

"No, uh, Henrietta's out of town at a conference this week, so it'll just be me." He had been dating Henrietta Blunt, who oversaw the local marsh on behalf of Wetlands Unlimited, since the spring, and despite Nurse Chaykowski's apparent advances, he had no interest in any other women.

"That's too bad. Perhaps we can have her over as well next time."

"Yes. Thank you . . . Doctor."

Dr. Maharaj waved as he continued down the hallway. Romanowski's brow was furrowed in concentration as he watched him, still seeking some sort of telltale sign regarding the doctor's identity.

"You have no idea which Dr. Maharaj you just agreed to eat dinner with, do you?" Nurse Chaykowski said.

"What makes you think that?" Romanowski asked, his eyes still on the doctor.

"Well, if you know so much, tell me. Who just invited you over for dinner: Harpreet or Bash?"

He turned to face her, his left eyebrow raised. "You're saying you can tell them apart?"

She sniffed in disdain. "Of course."

"How?"

"I'll tell you . . . under one condition."

"Oh yeah? What's that?"

She leaned forward and rested her chin on her hands, batting her eyelashes once again. "Did I ever tell you how much I love curry?"

Romanowski's nostrils flared. "Wait a second, I don't—"

"You do know where my house is, correct?"

"Yes, but—"

"Good. You can pick me up on Tuesday evening, 5:45 p.m. sharp."

Romanowski was about to refuse but then thought better of it, realizing he was trapped. It was either take Nurse Chaykowski to the dinner or admit his detective skills had failed, and there was no way he was doing the latter. He let out a huge sigh and then turned toward the door, having forgotten all about Dewey. All he was worried about now was how he was going to break the news to Henrietta.

§

Shivering in the crisp early morning air, sunglasses on and umbrella in hand, Dewey peered through the silver chain-link fence that surrounded the impound lot of Zee's Towing. He was chilled to the bone, having spent most of the night trudging down gravel roads, guided by moonlight and flashlight, digging randomly in various locations that felt vaguely familiar in relation to the night of the crash but finding nothing. In a daze from fatigue and post-concussion symptoms, after coming up empty, he began to wonder if he had dreamed the whole thing and that perhaps the hard-shell case was still where he could last recall seeing it: in the back seat of the station wagon. There was only one way to find out. It was his last stop before checking himself back into the hospital for some rest and recovery.

Squinting in the glare, he set his umbrella upside down in the snow. Just as he was about to scale the fence, Dewey heard a growl. It was followed by a flash of black-and-brown fur as a German shepherd roared out from between some snow-covered vehicles. It raced up to the fence barking as if it were going to run right through it, causing Dewey to take a cautious step back before it stopped, snarling as it paced up and down the opposite side of the fence, looking like it would enjoy nothing more than to sink its yellow teeth into Dewey's backside.

"Whoa, Sarge! Chill!" a voice said. Dewey looked toward the office and saw a squat, grizzled man in his late twenties approaching. He wore a greasy Saskatchewan Roughriders cap and smudged glasses. His Roughriders jacket was undone, and crumbs littered his white-and-green Roughriders T-shirt, as if he had just been disturbed from his breakfast, which appeared to have been a croissant and coffee, judging from the stains on his shirt that accompanied the flakes of pastry. But considering his overall appearance, the crumbs and stains could have just as easily been the remains of the previous day's breakfast, lunch, or supper.

"Don't mind the dog," the man said, wiping his mouth as he approached the fence. "The name's Corey, but people around here call me Zee. What can I do for you this fine morning?"

"You have my station wagon in there," Dewey said, pointing to it. The Fury's front end was crumpled due to the moose, and its windshield had a huge, star-shaped crack on the driver's side, presumably where Dewey's head had struck it.

Zee turned to look at it. "That your wagon?" He turned back to Dewey, looking him up and down. "Went moose huntin' with it, hey?" He chuckled at his own joke.

Dewey smiled weakly. "I guess you could say that."

"Lot of that these days. Bad for the drivers and bad for the moose but good for me." Zee gestured to a line of similarly damaged vehicles. "You blow it, I tow it. Ka-ching! Come to think of it, that would make a pretty good tagline for my company." He paused as he mulled over the idea.

"Uh, anyway," Dewey said, striving to redirect the conversation, "I, uh, I think I left something inside my car, and I was wondering if I could get it."

"Sorry, no can do," Zee said, snapping out of his daydream. "That there vehicle is what you call evidence."

"Excuse me?"

"Property of the RCMP," Zee said, emphasizing each letter of the abbreviation.

"It's not their property; it's mine," Dewey protested. "They can't just take my car from me. They haven't even pressed any charges."

"I don't know about all that, but I do know they can hold it temporarily until they answer a few questions about it. There's no way you're driving it out of here anyway. That beast is totaled. Be thankful. The moose put that hunk of junk out of its misery. Now you should at least get a decent insurance payment instead of having to drive around in that deathtrap."

"I don't want to drive the wagon. Like I said, I just want to look inside it. I won't take anything. I just want to see if my things are still in there."

Zee looked Dewey up and down, as if seeing him for the first time. He nodded at the umbrella. "What's with the getup?"

Dewey tapped his head—gently. "Concussion. From the accident. Makes me sensitive to light." He seized the opportunity to pick up the umbrella and shield his eyes again, instantly feeling a measure of relief.

"Where you from?" Zee asked.

"Saskatoon."

Zee nodded silently. "Riders fan?"

"Of course."

"Love the Riders," Zee said. "Hate Regina."

Dewey's eyes lit up. "Me too!"

Just then, Sarge whined, looking up at Zee with pleading eyes. He scowled at the dog. "What do you want? You already had your breakfast."

Dewey crouched down and held his hand up to the fence. "Nice doggy."

"I wouldn't do that if I were you," Zee warned. "Sarge can be—" Before he could finish, Sarge sniffed Dewey's mitt and then started licking it through the fence. "Well, I'll be," Zee said, watching in amazement. "Sarge hates everybody." He pushed his cap back on his head, revealing his greasy brown hair. "Say, you had breakfast yet? Because if you haven't, I still have a couple of croissants and some coffee, and maybe after that we can talk about you taking a peek inside that vehicle of yours."

Dewey stood up and smiled. "Sounds good to me."

§

Matt, Chad, and Andrew roared up to their first potential location, the Taylor boys riding double while

Andrew rode on his own sled. As their machines glided to a stop, they couldn't believe their eyes.

"It's perfect!" Matt said. And it was perfect. The ground sloped up and away from the road on the west side, and a line of trees along the ridge formed a perfect windbreak. As a result, a nice cornice had formed at the top, and the slope was covered with deep, soft snow.

"There's just one problem," Chad said. "Look." He pointed to a set of footprints leading up the slope. Actually, they were more like a set of deep holes. Whoever had set foot off the road had sunk up to their waist before thinking better of it and slithering across the snow. Not only did it mar the otherwise pristine white expanse, as the boys followed the trail up the slope with their eyes, right near a partially buried barbed-wire fence they saw something that caused their jaws to drop open: tunnels!

"What the heck?" Matt exclaimed. Without another word, he tore off his helmet and scrambled up the slope. The other two boys were right behind him. When they reached the tunnels, they sat back on their haunches in the snow, surveying the damage.

"It's ruined!" Matt said.

"Well, it's not ideal," Andrew admitted, "though we could always work around them."

"But who the heck would do such a thing?" Matt asked.

"It's not like we're the only ones who like digging snow tunnels," Chad said. "It could have been anyone. Some other kids maybe."

Matt looked back down toward the road. "But why here of all places?"

"Because it's a perfect spot," Andrew pointed out. "Just as we suspected."

"But look at these things," Matt said, turning back to the tunnels. "They're terrible. They don't go anywhere, and they're not connected. It's like whoever did it couldn't make up their mind on where to dig. They started one tunnel, dug for a bit, and then started another. Why couldn't they just dig one tunnel instead of ruining the entire ridge?"

"Maybe they got bored," Chad suggested, noting that all the tunnels tended to follow the fence line.

"Or maybe they did it on purpose to ruin it for us," Matt said, his eyes narrowing in suspicion.

The other two boys looked at him in confusion. "What on earth are you talking about?" Chad asked. "Who would waste their time ruining a perfect snow maze location? Are you saying you think we have some competition?"

"No, not competition. A saboteur."

"What?" Chad said. "Who?"

"Who do you think?" Matt asked. "Who isn't here right now but should be?"

Chad's eyes widened in surprise. "You're saying you think Dean came out here in the middle of the night and ruined this location just because you don't want him to ask Joyce to the Valentine's Day dance?"

"Well, doesn't that sound like something he would do?"

"It sounds like something his mother would do," Andrew remarked.

"Good point," Chad admitted. "But it's still highly unlikely."

"Well, there's only one way to find out," Matt said, sliding back down the ridge.

"Wait a second, what are you talking about?" Chad asked. "And where are you going?"

"Where do you think? To talk to Dean."

"But that's crazy!" Chad called after his brother. "Dean didn't do this. Besides, we've got a ton of scouting to do!"

"There's no use scouting if Dean's going ahead of us and ruining everything," Matt said. "I'm going to nip this thing in the bud."

As Chad and Andrew watched in disbelief, Matt jumped onto the Taylor boys' sled, fired it up, and took off back the way they had come. Chad shook his head slowly as he watched Matt drive along the ditch toward town. "My little brother is crazy," he said.

Andrew sniffed. "You're only realizing that now?"

9

An Unexpected Partner

When Clive left Earl's headquarters in search of Dewey, he was on top of the world. With a new car, a wad of cash in his pocket, the open road before him, and the promise of virtually unlimited riches on the horizon, it should have been the best trip of his life. But just over twenty-four hours into the journey, he couldn't have been more miserable.

"I said turn the heat up, not down! I'm freezing over here!"

Clive glared at the young woman in his passenger seat and then cranked the heat with a vicious flick of his wrist.

"Not on my face! I can't stand air blowing on my face. Put it on the floor! My feet are like icicles."

With a low growl of frustration, Clive shifted the heat to "floor/defrost" instead of "panel."

"Better?" he growled, not caring if it was.

"A bit," she said, shivering as she zipped her coat right up to her chin. "But as soon as we hit the next town, we need to stop. I have to go to the bathroom."

The woman in the passenger seat was none other than Amber Paproski, a.k.a. Dewey's girlfriend—ex-girlfriend, actually, as Clive had recently learned. How she had ended up in Clive's car and why he had agreed to bring her along on his journey was a sequence of events that he was still struggling to understand.

Clive had begun his search for Dewey by scouring his various haunts throughout Saskatoon—Dewey's apartment, his favorite watering hole, and his favorite pool hall. He had also paid a visit to some of Dewey's lowlife friends. Not only was there no sign that Dewey had returned home after his trip—the pile of mail on the floor just inside his door, consisting mainly of overdue bills, was proof of that—his friends claimed not to have seen him. Despite his contemptuous view of Dewey's cronies, Clive was inclined to believe them, if only because they knew all too well the consequences of lying to Clive—or Earl. The troglodytes did give him one potentially useful piece of information though. For reasons that befuddled Clive to no end, the pond scum known as Dewey Biggs had somehow convinced a woman to date him, though, not unexpectedly from Clive's point of view, the relationship had come to a speedy and explosive end.

As eager as he was to hit the road, Clive decided to make one final stop before leaving town, the seedy convenience store where Dewey's jilted ex-lover worked, to see if he could glean any more information from her.

Amber was only too eager to dish dirt on Dewey, which instantly raised Clive's estimation of her. But before he knew it, she had quit her job on the spot, loaded up with every form of junk food and soft drink imaginable, and plunked herself in the passenger seat of his car, insisting she join him on his search.

To convince him of her worth, Amber claimed to have a sixth sense when it came to Dewey. She said all she had to do was close her eyes, put her hand to her forehead, and ask, "What would Dewey do?" Before she knew it, her woman's intuition would lead her straight to that "scum-sucking, conniving little rat," as Amber referred to him. Clive had no idea what Dewey had done to make her so angry at him, nor did he care, but as soon as they pulled away from the convenience store, she wasted no time reciting a litany of complaints against the little twerp as she narrated her tale of romantic woe.

Despite her claim to have a sixth sense when it came to Dewey, so far all she'd done was establish why Dewey had been right to break up with her. Hours in a car with Amber's nonstop babble and her singing along with virtually every song that came on the radio was unbearable. Clive had no idea how Dewey had managed to last four months. Now all he could think about was how to get rid of her, which he planned to do at their next stop. The moment she was safely ensconced inside the gas station bathroom, he would put the pedal to the metal, never to see or hear from her again.

"No, don't stop here. Stop at that one," Amber said, pointing to the Husky station across the highway as Clive rolled the New Yorker to a stop outside an Esso station.

"What's wrong with this one?" Clive asked, pressing the button to roll down his window as the gas jockey approached.

"Their bathrooms are horrible. And besides, they don't sell my favorite soft drink."

Clive cast a skeptical look at the pile of soda cans, empty chip bags, and candy bar wrappers on the floor at her feet. "You need another soft drink?" He wondered how she managed to maintain her trim figure with such a colossal intake of garbage.

She scowled at him. "What are you implying? You have something to say about what I drink?"

"No, I just—"

"'Cause Dewey used to harp about that all the time until I—"

"Fill it up, sir?" the gas jockey asked, steam coming out of the mouth hole of his balaclava in the cold air. Clive looked at Amber, who crossed her arms and glared at him.

"No Husky, no Dewey."

Clive sighed, willing to do anything at that point just to be rid of her. He turned back to the gas jockey with an apologetic look. "Sorry," he said, "I guess we're still making up our minds."

He rolled up his window and then eased away from the pumps. The gas jockey shook his head at their retreating vehicle and then moved on to serve another customer.

"You're not embarrassing at all," Clive remarked, looking both ways before crossing the highway.

"What do you have to be embarrassed about?" Amber asked. "You're never going to see that jerk again."

"What makes you think he's a jerk?" Clive asked. "There is such a thing as human decency, you know." Seeing a break in traffic. He hit the gas, and the New Yorker surged across the highway.

"Hmph," Amber said. "As if you'd know anything about it. Decency is the first thing that goes out the window when people start working for Earl."

"Just be quick in there," Clive said as he pulled up to the pumps. "We still have a lot of ground to cover. And you might want to unload some of this trash while we're here," he added, indicating the pile of rubbish at her feet.

"You don't like it? Do something about it yourself, Jeeves," she said with a guffaw as she opened her door and then hurried toward the station. She had taken to calling him "Jeeves" almost immediately upon hearing his accent, the slang term for a butler or valet, yet another aspect of her personality that rankled Clive. He waited until she was inside and then restarted the New Yorker. He went to pull out but then slammed on his brakes, nearly hitting the gas jockey, who had approached his vehicle from the front to see if he wanted a fill-up.

Clive hurriedly rolled down his window and stuck his head out. "Sorry about that, mate. Changed my mind at the last minute. In a bit of a hurry to get back on the road."

"Not with that you aren't," the gas jockey said, pointing to the front-left side of Clive's vehicle.

Clive tried to stretch his head out the window to see what he was pointing at, but his seatbelt held him back. "With what?" he asked.

"Your tire," the gas jockey said. "It's almost flat."

"Are you kidding me?" Clive growled in frustration, casting a furtive glance back at the gas station's front doors. "How bad is it?"

"Bad."

"Bad enough I can't make it to the next town?"

The gas jockey shrugged. "That all depends on how many sparks you want to send up along the way."

Clive let out a low growl. "Do you have an air compressor?"

"On the side of the building," the gas jockey said, pointing to it.

Clive looked at the front door of the gas station again. Still no sign of Amber. With any luck, he could park the vehicle out of sight to fill up the tire. When she came out, she would assume he had left her and probably go back inside in a huff to call someone to pick her up. Then he could sneak around behind the building, cut through the small town to make some inquiries about Dewey, and then hit the road, with Amber none the wiser.

Giddy at the thought of finally being free of her, Clive parked by the air compressor, then jumped out and grabbed the hose. He spun the cover off the valve stem and put the hose on it. But when he pressed the lever to put air into the tire, nothing happened.

"What the . . .?" He looked up and realized the compressor required him to insert a dime for it to operate. "Are you freakin' kidding me?" He dove into his car and scoured the seats and the glovebox for some change. Just when he was about to give up, he spotted a dime glistening under the pile of garbage on the passenger seat floor. It probably belonged to Amber, but he deserved far more than ten cents for having had to put up with her for so long.

He leaped out of the car and slammed the dime into the machine, then hit the button to get the air flowing. The compressor roared to life, causing Clive to cringe. What if she heard it?

With no time to worry about that, he jammed the hose onto his valve stem. Seconds later, his tire was properly inflated. Why it had lost so much air was a question he would have to deal with later. First things first. He had to get out of there.

Clive threw the hose back onto the compressor, not bothering to wind it up properly, then got back into his car. He slammed it into "drive" and was just about to nail the gas when he looked up and hit on the brakes in horror. Standing in front of the car was Amber, a huge bag of junk food in hand and a vicious scowl on her face.

"Going somewhere?" she asked, biting into a Hot Rod and chewing it savagely. Clive sighed and then leaned over to open the passenger door for her.

"A door is ajar," the car said in its mechanical voice. "A door is ajar."

Though the thought of a talking car had excited Clive when Earl had first handed him the keys, now he never wanted to hear that voice again.

10

A Dead End

Matt brought the Arctic Cat to a stop beside the high school. Technically speaking, snowmobiles weren't allowed within town limits, but the RCMP tended to turn a blind eye to such things if people drove them respectfully, though Matt had hardly done that in his haste to track down Dean.

He hopped off the machine and then took off his helmet and set it on the seat, only to have it roll off into the snow. Not bothering to pick it up, he stomped past a plywood sign with

"Snow Sculptures" and an arrow spray-painted on it, heading toward an open area between the main school building and two outbuildings.

"Dean Muller!" he yelled as he approached a shantytown that had been hastily constructed out of plywood, two-by-fours, and blue tarps to shield the snow sculptures from prying eyes.

"Moo!" a male voice said.

"Moo!" a female voice replied.

"Moo!"

Matt stopped in his tracks and looked back at the sign.

It said "Snow Sculptures," but why did it sound like he was about to enter a meeting of the local 4-H club?

Matt's question was answered when Ben Somerville emerged from the plywood and two-by-four structure, his blue toque no doubt concealing a chronic case of bedhead.

"Moo!" Ben said when he saw Matt, the cow-obsessed kid's typical greeting whenever he met anyone of the human or bovine species.

"What's going on in there?" Matt asked, still unsure if he was at the right spot. Just then, a girl came out behind Ben dressed in a pink one-piece snowsuit.

"Moo," she said, causing Matt to roll his eyes. Recently, Ben had found his soulmate in the form of Zoey Barnes, a girl who was just as obsessed with cows as he was. If they had entered the snow sculpture contest, there was no doubt in Matt's mind what they were creating.

"Can someone please tell me if this is where the snow sculptures are being made?"

"Yeah, what's it to you, Taylor?" Mr. Karky asked as he came out the side door of the gym and headed toward the structure, the huge pom-pom on his homemade knitted toque bobbing as he walked. He was the staff member assigned to oversee the contest. "I didn't see your name on the sign-up sheet."

"That's because I didn't sign up for the contest," Matt said. "I'm here to talk to Dean Muller. Is he in there?"

"What do I look like, his babysitter?" Mr. Karky asked as he headed into the ramshackle structure.

Matt held his hands up in frustration. "But I just want to—"

"Muller! Someone's here to see you!" Mr. Karky yelled. Then he stuck his head out of the structure's doorway.

"By the way, Taylor, if you're not sculpting, stay out." He thumped a sign that said, "Snow Sculptors Only" beside the doorway. "I catch you in here before the day of the contest, and—"

"I know, I know," Matt said. "Detention for a week."

"Two weeks if you interrupt me like that again."

Matt hung his head. "Sorry."

A moment later, Dean peeked out and then ducked back inside.

"Dean!" Matt said. "Come out here and talk."

Dean peeked out again and then emerged fully from the structure. "Sorry," he said. "I was worried you were my mom coming to pick me up already."

"Do I look like your mom?"

Dean clasped his chin with his thumb and forefinger and pretended to look Matt up and down. "Well, now that you mention it—"

"Knock it off, and tell me where you were last night."

Dean lowered his hand, a shocked expression stealing over his face. "Excuse me? Was I supposed to be somewhere?"

"Just answer the question," Matt said, at the end of his patience.

"I don't know," Dean replied, his mind racing. "I was . . . I was at home. I watched a movie on TV with my dad."

"Oh yeah? What movie?"

"King Kong. The 1976 remake with Jeff Bridges and Jessica Lange. It was awful. But the special effects were pretty cool."

Matt scowled. "That movie wasn't on TV last night."

"I know. We rented a video. I've been wanting to watch it forever, but what a waste of money."

"Do you have a receipt?"

"No, I don't have a receipt. My dad paid for it. Wait a second, why are you asking me all these questions?"

"Because we found the perfect location for a snow maze this morning."

"Oh yeah? That's great." Suddenly, Dean realized Matt had an angry expression on his face. "It is great, right?"

"It would have been," Matt said, "if someone hadn't beaten us to it—and ruined it."

Dean frowned. "I don't understand. You mean . . . wait a second, you think I went there ahead of you and wrecked it? Are you kidding me? I don't even like building snow tunnels."

"If not you then who?" Matt asked, his anger diminishing slightly as the logic of Dean's argument began to sink in.

Before Dean could answer, a female voice floated toward them. "Oh, Deanie!" It prompted an immediate scowl on Dean's freckled face.

"I told you never to call me that!" he said, glancing back over his shoulder.

Joy emerged from the snow sculpture structure, clipboard in hand, a bright orange scarf wrapped around her neck, which accentuated her beaming face. "Good morning, Matt. If you're here to join the contest, I'm sorry to say it, but we're full up."

"No, he's not here to join the contest," Dean said. "In fact, he was just leaving. Weren't you, Matt?"

"Moo," Ben said. He and Zoey had stood by listening to the exchange. Matt turned to look at him. Ben had his arms crossed, a scowl on his face. Zoey looked at Ben and then mimicked his stance and his expression, throwing in another angry "Moo" for good measure.

"Yes, I guess I'll leave you lovebirds alone for now," Matt said.

"We're not lovebirds!" Dean said, glowering at Joy to make sure she got his point. She continued to beam at him, not at all deterred by his lack of reciprocation.

"But if I find out you're lying, Dean . . ."

"Seriously, Matt, use your head," Dean said. "I don't want anything to do with your stupid snow maze—or you for that matter." With that, he disappeared back inside the shantytown.

"Dean, wait!" Matt said, realizing he had crossed the line. "I'm sorry! I just—" When Dean failed to emerge, Matt hung his head and then turned and trudged back to his snowmobile.

Ben and Zoey watched him go. Ben shook his head in disgust and then turned to Zoey. "Moo?"

She nodded vigorously in agreement and then glared at Matt's retreating form. "Moo."

§

"So anyway, I sez to this guy, 'Your dad musta taught you to use the right tool for the job, 'cause you're a tool all right, and you're doing a terrible job!'"

Dewey forced a smile that came out looking more like a grimace as he tried to stomach another sip of stale coffee. He was sitting in an old, ragged office chair across from Zee, enduring yet another of the tow truck driver's tedious stories. The chair's greasy brown seat was held together more by frayed silver duct tape than fabric, which was a good metaphor for Zee's Towing as a whole. The business appeared to thrive merely because it was the only towing company within a thirty-mile radius, not because it was a paragon of professionalism, customer service, or, judging by the office and its owner, cleanliness.

"He wasn't having none of that," Zee said. "It was thirty below, the snow was blowing like crazy, and he wasn't even wearing a jacket, but he hauled off and—"

"I don't mean to butt in," Dewey lied (after nearly forty-five minutes of Zee's stories, that was exactly what he meant to do), "but about my station wagon, do you mind if I take a look at it? Like I said, I don't even need to go inside it. Just peek through the windows."

Zee downed the last of what Dewey estimated to be his eighth Styrofoam cup of coffee, each one augmented by several heaping spoonfuls of sugar and powdered coffee creamer, and then wiped his mouth and turned to a rack of keys hanging behind his desk. "You know what? You seem like a pretty decent guy. I don't see how one little look could hurt."

Moments later, they were trudging across the snow-filled lot, Dewey's head beginning to throb almost immediately as the sunlight reflected off the snow and into his eyes. He tried to adjust his umbrella and his sunglasses to reduce the glare.

"Quite the gas guzzler you have there," Zee said as they approached the station wagon. "Or I should say 'had.' Must have been quite the knock on the noggin," he added, indicating the star-shaped crack on the driver's side of the windshield.

"Yes," Dewey said, his head smarting even more at the sight of it.

"Tell you what," Zee said. "If you promise not to take anything out of it, I'll even let you take a peek inside." He pulled out the keys and unlocked the driver's door, then opened it and stepped aside, so Dewey could get in. "Make it quick though," Zee added, glancing around. "The last thing I need is the cops on my case. Did I ever tell you about the time I was in high school and—"

Without realizing he had done it, Dewey slammed the door, no doubt subconsciously trying to shut Zee out. He opened his mouth to apologize, but Zee waved him off. "Good idea! Makes it less obvious!" Apparently, he didn't realize his shouting had the opposite effect.

As Zee kept an eye out for the police, Dewey immediately looked in the back seat. Much to his chagrin, the hard-shell case was nowhere in sight. He peeked under the seats as well, but there was no sign of it. Only two possibilities remained. First, and most frightening, the RCMP had it. However, if that were true, they would have opened it by now, and if they had, Romanowski would have arrested Dewey already. Unless they hadn't opened it because they were waiting for a warrant or something like that. But considering Romanowski's suspicions about the mismatched license plates and Dewey in general, they would have wasted no time opening the case if they had it in their possession. That left the other option. Somewhere not far away, the case was buried in the snow, waiting for Dewey to find it. All he had to do was figure out where.

To help jog his memory, he put his hands on the steering wheel and closed his eyes, trying to recall the events of that night once again . . .

§

Around the same time Dewey was on his "vision quest" inside the Fury, Matt was just settling down with a cup of hot chocolate in the tree house when the structure started to vibrate due to someone climbing the ladder. Moments later, the trapdoor popped open.

"I thought we'd find you up here," Chad said as he

clambered inside, followed closely by Andrew.

"What's up, guys?" Matt said. "Sorry to ditch you, but I had to get to the bottom of who made those tunnels."

"And?" Chad said, raising his right eyebrow in anticipation as he unzipped his jacket.

Matt dropped his eyes to the floor. "I think I owe Dean an apology."

"Well, you'd better not waste any time doing it," Chad said as he kicked off his boots.

Matt looked up at his brother. "Why's that? By the way, how'd the rest of the scouting go?"

Chad exchanged a look with Andrew. "Well, that's the thing. We've got some good news and some bad news."

"What's the good news?" Matt asked, his eyes lighting up.

Chad looked at Andrew to see if he wanted to reply, but Andrew motioned for him to speak. Chad turned back to his brother. "The good news is we've found the perfect spot."

"That's great!" Matt replied. "Whose land is it on?"

"That's the bad news," Andrew said, pulling out his map and spreading it across the table. Matt stood up and leaned over it, his eyes honing in on where Andrew's finger was pointing.

"A. Muller," Matt said, reading the name of the person who owned the quarter section. "Who's th—" He stopped short as his eyes widened with realization. "No . . ."

"That's right," Chad said, nodding grimly. "The land belongs to Dean's mother."

11

Checking In

Earl was losing his patience. Not only had that dimwit Dewey gone missing with his precious cargo, now Clive, Earl's most trusted employee, had disappeared too. Over twenty-four hours had passed, and not a peep from the AWOL Englishman. It was starting to feel like a horror movie, with one person disappearing after the next. Earl could only imagine what would happen if he sent someone else looking for Clive and another buffoon looking for that person and so on and so on. Pretty soon his entire organization would be missing, and Earl would be left all alone in his office with no one to do his dirty work—or make his tea. Speaking of which . . .

Earl snatched a copper bell off his desk and rang it with frustration. "Meinhardt! You're late—again!"

Momentarily, Meinhardt, one of Earl's oldest employees, kicked his door open and then tried to dart inside before it closed again, tea tray in hand. He didn't quite make it. The door struck the tray as he tried to spin out of the way, causing him to slop tea everywhere and sending shortbread cookies flying.

"Oh, for the love of Pete!" Earl exclaimed, slamming

the bell onto his desk. "Grab a brain, Meinhardt! No one else around here appears to be taking them."

"Sorry, sir," Meinhardt said. He scooped the shortbread cookies off the floor, dusted them off, then put them back on the tray and made a show of trying to arrange things nicely before he crossed the office and set the tray on Earl's desk. He stood back and clasped his hands in front of him like a footman, waiting for Earl to dig in. Meinhardt was a small man with about as many teeth as he had toes, but that never stopped him from smiling, especially when he was nervous. And being around Earl always made him nervous.

"What are you grinning about?" Earl barked. "You think that tea's going to pour itself?"

"Oh, sorry, sir." Meinhardt's smile broadened even further as he leaped into action. He grabbed the teapot and sloshed some tea into Earl's cup, spilling some onto the saucer. Earl huffed in disdain as Meinhardt picked up the bowl of sugar and snatched a cube out of it with his black, greasy fingers, holding it over the cup and offering Earl a gap-toothed smile. "One lump or two, sir?"

"How many times do I have to tell you I don't take sugar in my tea, you nitwit?" Earl knocked the sugar cubes out of Meinhardt's hand and then grabbed his teacup and saucer, accidentally spilling some tea on himself in the process. "Now look what you've done!"

Ever eager to please, Meinhardt snatched a cloth napkin off the tray and began patting the tea stain on Earl's shirt. "Terribly sorry, sir, if you just—"

"Get your hands off me!" Earl said, batting him away. "And while you're at it—"

Before Earl could finish, his phone rang. He picked up the receiver on the first ring. "If this isn't Dewey or Clive, so help me . . ."

"It's Clive, sir," his trusty employee replied.

"Why haven't you checked in?" Earl snapped. "What the heck is going on out there?"

Clive shivered in a phone booth as he looked back at the New Yorker. Exhaust fumes swirled around the vehicle as it sat running nearby. Amber was in the passenger seat singing with gusto along with a song on the radio. Thankfully, Clive was unable to hear her over the sound of the vehicle and the wind. The last few hours had been bad enough. He'd never look at American Top Forty the same way again. While he still planned on ditching her at some point, even though she irritated him to no end, a recent development had shown she may just have some use after all.

"It's . . . complicated, sir," Clive said.

"Complicated? What's complicated about it?" Earl said. "You were supposed to check in every twelve hours, and this is the first I've heard from you. I was starting to think you and Dewey were in cahoots."

"Not at all, sir, not at all. It's just more work than I anticipated. And I wanted to wait until I at least had some news." Even though Clive still intended to leave Earl's employ, he had decided to keep checking in for as long as possible to avoid raising Earl's suspicion.

"Where are you?"

Clive was about to reply when he stopped short. He had already been to so many little towns, and Amber's singing and nonstop prattle had so addled his mind that he had completely lost track of his location. He looked outside the phone booth to see if he could spot any indication of where he was.

"Actually, I don't know, sir, I—"

"You don't know? How on earth could you not know where you are?"

"I apologize, sir, but I've never been down this highway before, and the map is back in the car. I'm outside a service station by the highway, and—"

"Never mind that. Have you seen any sign of Dewey?"

"Not yet, sir, but I'm confident it's only a matter of time. I've been asking about him at gas stations, hospitals, motels, pool halls, pubs, even police stations."

"Police stations! What are you trying to do, bring the heat down on us?"

"No, sir. I came up with a story, saying Dewey is my little brother, and we had a falling out. He ran away, so I'm out here on the road looking for him. They eat it up every time."

"Hmph. And?"

"Nothing so far. But I've put up photos of him in every post office with your phone number on the bottom."

"My phone number? Are you kidding me?"

Clive hesitated. "I'm sorry, sir, but I didn't know what other number to use."

"Forget it," Earl said. "Maybe it's no big deal. Anyway, you won't find Dewey by standing around yakking. Get back on the road, and don't wait so long before checking in next time, got it?"

"Yes, sir."

"And hurry back. This tea Meinhardt's making me is awful!"

"I'm terribly sorry to hear it, sir."

Earl sighed, almost making Clive feel guilty about his plan to betray him. "It's not your fault. Just find Dewey, and everything will be fine."

"Certainly, sir. You can count on me."

Clive hung up the phone and looked back at the car. Amber had broken into another song, this time using a Mr. Big chocolate bar as a microphone. Now that he was no longer on the phone, he could just make out the words to a hit by the Fine Young Cannibals: "She drives me crazy! Like no one else!"

He shook his head. Truer words had not been spoken—or sung.

12

More Bad News

Dewey opened his eyes and released his hands from the Plymouth Fury's steering wheel, his palms white from gripping it so hard. Try as he might, he couldn't remember anything specific about the location of the hard-shell case. All he saw was a jumble of images—the snowplow, the blowing snow, the moose antlers, barbed wire, and his padlock—but nothing that could lead him to its actual location.

Sighing in defeat, he was about to resign himself to another long, cold night of searching when he happened to glance up and see Zee cleaning his greasy fingernails outside the vehicle as he waited for Dewey to finish. Of course! Zee had towed his vehicle after the accident. He would know exactly where it had occurred. Once Dewey knew that, it would be a simple matter of backtracking toward the gravel road where he had buried the case. He fumbled with the door handle. He couldn't get out of the Fury fast enough.

§

"The land belongs to Dean's mother?" Matt said, sinking back into a chair as he processed the news. "How on earth does she own a quarter section of farmland? She's not a farmer."

"No, but her father is, and it looks like she doesn't just own a quarter," Andrew said, pulling out the map and showing it to Matt. "As you can see here, she owns the entire section. Maybe her dad put some of his land into her name as an inheritance thing. Or maybe it has something to do with taxes. Whatever the case, if we're going to build a snow maze there, we'll have to go through her first."

Matt looked up at Andrew and Chad in alarm. "Then we'll find another place. Or go back to some of the places we rejected. They weren't so bad. Or maybe we can go back to that original gully where I first got the idea. We can talk to the landowner, offer him a bigger cut to . . ." His voice trailed off as Andrew and Chad shook their heads. "What's the matter?" Matt asked. "Those are good ideas."

"Actually, they're not," Chad said. "First of all, we rejected all the other locations for good reason. Even the one with the snow tunnels already built. Andrew and I thought we could work around them, but after doing a depth test, we realized there wasn't as much snow there as we thought. Turns out that beneath the snow is a rock pile, which is probably why whoever dug the original tunnels kept stopping and restarting. He or she kept running into rocks. As for the other locations, you were there, and you know why we rejected them. I hadn't thought about the original spot though." He looked at Andrew to get his input and was met by another head shake.

"The landowner was pretty adamant about it," Andrew said. "We can try, but I highly doubt we'll be able to convince him to put his neck on the line for us. Plus, there's also the access issue. So, unless you want to start looking for locations even farther out of town, this is our only option. And it's a great option. The best of the bunch." He looked at Chad, who nodded in agreement before turning to his brother.

"You should see it, Matt. It's perfect."

Matt scoffed. "I don't need to see it. If that farmer won't put his neck on the line for us, do you really think Mrs. Muller will? Not a chance, especially once she finds out I'm involved. Besides, I just majorly ticked off Dean, so there's no way he'll go to bat for us, not that it would do any good the way she railroads him all the time."

Chad and Andrew exchanged a look. "Actually," Chad said, "we've already given that problem some thought, and we think we've come up with a solution."

"Oh yeah?" Matt said, eyeing them skeptically. "What?"

Chad turned to Andrew and nodded for him to break the news. "I hate to say it," Andrew said, "but if this project is going to go ahead . . . you can't be part of it."

Matt's eyes widened in anger and surprise. "What?"

§

Staff Sergeant Romanowski sat at his desk in the RCMP detachment, musing. He had all sorts of cases he should have been investigating, including Dewey's whereabouts, but only one thing was occupying his mind: his dinner at Dr. Maharaj's house. Not only was he unsure which doctor had invited him over, his only way of finding out for sure was to bring Nurse Chaykowski as his date. Although he had never viewed her as anything more than an acquaintance, someone he had met in the course of carrying out his duties as a peace officer, it was clear from their latest interaction that Nurse Chaykowski saw things differently. If he went through with it, even if he kept things platonic, not only would that encourage her advances, he shuddered to think what Henrietta would do when she found out. And she would find out. Milligan Creek was so small that he'd be surprised if she didn't know about it already, even though she was out of town for a week-long conference, where she was presenting a paper on wetland carbon sequestration and nutrient accumulation, whatever that was. All he knew was that she had been preparing it for months.

That did it. It was time to nip things in the bud. He'd call Dr. Maharaj and postpone things until Henrietta was back in town. And then he'd—

He paused, his hand hovering over the phone. But which Dr. Maharaj should he call? He thought about simply phoning the clinic and leaving a message, but surely the receptionist would ask which doctor he was referring to, and then what would he say? And what if Nurse Chaykowski herself picked up the phone?

Before he could figure a way out of his dilemma, the intercom on his desk beeped.

"Yes?" Romanowski said, irritated at the interruption.

"Call for you on line two," his receptionist said.

"Who is it?"

"Why, it's Miss Henrietta Blunt, sir."

Romanowski swallowed hard, ignoring the sarcasm in her voice. "OK, put her through."

§

"You know, Corey—I mean Zee," Dewey said as he stumbled out of the station wagon, suddenly cringing in pain and shielding his eyes from the sunlight. Zee handed him his umbrella, which brought instant relief. "Thanks. Anyway, as I was saying, you towed this station wagon here from the accident scene, correct?"

"I sure did," Zee said. "You think I would trust anyone else to drive my truck?"

"No, of course not," Dewey replied. "Anyway, I was just wondering, I'm having a bit of a hard time remembering that night, and I wondered if revisiting the scene of the accident might, you know," he tapped the side of his head, trying not to wince at the pain it caused, "jog my memory."

Zee shrugged. "I'm no expert, but maybe it would."

Dewey nodded, waiting for Zee to pick up the hint. "If only my station wagon weren't all smashed up and the police hadn't impounded it," he said when it became apparent that Zee wasn't getting the message, "I could drive there myself."

Zee looked at the wagon and nodded. "Yep, you sure did a number on it. And you think your wagon looks bad? You shoulda seen that moose! Splat!" He splayed his fingers in the air to illustrate. "You know, some people eat roadkill like that. Don't think I wasn't tempted to cut off a steak or two while the carcass was still steaming."

"Yeah, I'll bet," Dewey said. "Well, thanks for breakfast and for showing me my vehicle. Guess I'll be on my way."

"Hey, wait a second," Zee said, a thought striking him. "I could take you out to the scene of the accident."

Dewey stopped and turned back. "Really?" he said as if the thought had just occurred to him too. "That would be great!"

Zee smiled. "Heck, what are friends for? Besides, if the conservation officers haven't gotten their hands on that moose yet, maybe it's not too late to get those steaks." He rubbed his hands together in anticipation.

§

Staff Sergeant Romanowski paused to mentally prepare himself and then picked up the receiver. "Henrietta, hello! What a nice surprise. It's so great to hear from you. In fact, I was just—" He stopped and listened as she talked over him. "Oh, so you won't be home until the weekend now? Why? What are you—" He stopped and listened as she cut him off again. "Oh, that sounds like a fantastic opportunity. But how can you study anything underwater if the lake is frozen? Oh, remote-sensing technology? What's that? A mini-submarine? You're going to go underwater in a mini-submarine? In February? But isn't that . . . oh, a remote-control submarine. Very cool!"

As she continued her explanation, he sat back in his chair and idly flipped through his Garfield desktop calendar, which Henrietta had given him as a stocking stuffer the previous Christmas. "What am I doing this coming Tuesday?" he replied when she was finished, not sure why she would ask him such a random question. "Oh, uh, nothing special," he said, suddenly losing the courage to tell her the truth.

He stopped on the calendar page where he had already marked his dinner date with Dr. Maharaj. It featured Garfield hugging his archrival, Odie, whose red tongue hung out and made the shape of a heart. It made Romanowski feel even guiltier for lying to her, but there was no way he was going to tell her he was planning to go out for dinner with Nurse Chaykowski, even if it was happening against his will. "Maybe I'll rent a movie, order some take-out . . ." His voice trailed off as the date on the calendar finally registered in his brain: February 14. Then his eyebrows shot up. Valentine's Day? He had just agreed to have dinner with Dr. Maharaj and his wife and Nurse Chaykowski on Valentine's Day?

He dropped the calendar in alarm. It fell open to a page that featured Garfield glowering as he clutched a baseball bat under a thought bubble that said, "I hate Mondays." As Romanowski stared at it, Garfield's face morphed into Henrietta's and the word "Mondays" transformed into "Richard" as he imagined how angry she would be once she discovered he was two-timing her—even though he had been tricked into it. Romanowski hadn't dated anyone for so long that he had completely forgotten about Valentine's Day. Now not only had he forgotten to plan something special for Henrietta or buy her a gift, he would be spending the evening with another woman. How was he going to get himself out of this situation? He was a police officer, not a relationship guru. Couldn't they give him a simpler problem to solve, like a robbery or a murder?

"I can't wait to see you either, Henrietta," he said as his attention returned to the conversation. "Well, enjoy the rest of the conference. I can't wait to hear all about it!" He smiled as hard as he could, hoping the shape of his lips was powerful enough to compensate for the lack of enthusiasm in his voice.

§

"Let me get this straight," Matt said, still dumbfounded by Andrew's words. "The snow maze was my idea, but I'm not allowed to participate?"

"Well, not officially," Andrew clarified.

Matt gave him a stunned look. "What the heck does that mean?"

"It means Mrs. Muller can't know it's your idea or that

you're going to help build it," Chad said as he took a chair, realizing this was going to be a long conversation.

"But that's ridiculous," Matt protested. "If you're involved, I'm involved. That's how these things work."

"Not if you're sick," Andrew said, sitting down beside Chad.

Matt turned to him. "What, are you two going to poison me or something?"

"We were thinking more along the lines of bronchitis," Chad said. "Or pneumonia."

Matt gawked at the other boys in disbelief. "You want me to risk my life and contract a deadly disease just so we can build a stupid snow maze?"

"Oh," Chad said, "so the snow maze is stupid now?"

"No! It's just—"

"You don't actually have to be sick," Andrew explained. "Just pretend. Or at the very least, we just need to give Mrs. Muller the impression you're sick."

"What if she talks to our parents? And she will talk to our parents."

Andrew shrugged. "Then you'll have to give them that impression too."

"And if Mom and Dad want to take me to the doctor?"

"That's where your skills as an actor come in," Chad said. "Take things right up to the line, but don't cross it."

"For how long?"

Andrew shrugged. "For as long as it takes us to build the maze."

Matt fell silent as he pondered the situation. "OK, say I go along with this crazy idea—and it is crazy, by the way—when am I supposed to help dig?"

"We were thinking you could take the night shift," Andrew said.

"Are you kidding me?" Matt exclaimed. "Go out there at night? On my own? Then I'd catch pneumonia for sure. Besides, how would I get there? It's not like I can pull out of the yard on the snowmobile after dark without Mom and Dad hearing me."

Chad and Andrew exchanged a look. They hadn't thought about the transportation issue.

"Maybe you could do it during the day then," Chad said. "Tell Mom and Dad you're going to Andrew or Dean's house, and then you can actually join up with us."

Matt shook his head. "No way. It would only be a matter of time before they found out. Our parents talk to each other way too much. And if I'm sick, there's no way they'll want me spreading it."

"You could say you were going to the library to do homework," Andrew suggested. Matt and Chad both stared at him in disbelief. His face reddened slightly as he shrugged. "It was just a suggestion."

"I have a much better idea," Matt said. He leaned forward in his chair as his mind churned with possibilities. "And it also involves giving Mom and Dad 'an impression' of something."

"Oh yeah? What's that?" Chad asked.

Matt grinned as he jabbed his brother in the chest with his index finger. "That you're me, and I'm you."

Chad rubbed his chest as he looked at Andrew, and then they both looked at Matt in confusion. "What?"

13

Clueless

Clive had never been a patient man, but his time on the road with Amber had pushed his tolerance level to heretofore unrealized limits. From her shrill voice to her ever-fluctuating body temperature to her penchant for all manner of junk food to her choice of music to her incessant requests for bathroom breaks, Clive was slowly but surely losing his mind. He'd been tempted to ditch her numerous times, his ultimate fantasy being to watch her tumble out the passenger door and into the snow-filled ditch at the relatively gentle speed of five miles per hour, surrounded by a cloud of food wrappers and empty soda cans. As appealing as that image was, despite his increasing irritation with her, Clive had come to see Amber as a vital link in his search for Dewey, and as time wore on, perhaps his only hope.

True to her word, each time they pulled into a new town, no matter how big or how small, while Clive insisted on going through his routine of consulting with gas station attendants, bartenders, fast-food servers, and the police while also putting up posters of Dewey all over town, all she had to do was close her eyes, put her hand to her forehead, and ask, "What would Dewey do?", and she would lead Clive straight to a clue that indicated whether Dewey had been there or not.

At first Clive was skeptical of her so-called psychic abilities, but in town after town, after going through her routine and making a prediction—usually prefaced by at least one service station bathroom break—they would arrive at the site, and sure enough, the evidence she had predicted would be there. The clues included everything from initials carved into a military cenotaph to library books about Saskatchewan placed in reverse alphabetical order to gas station receipts pinned to post office bulletin boards to an empty beer bottle stuck into a six-pack at the back of a shelf in the liquor store, cap on and all.

Not only was the sheer variety of clues baffling, she also claimed they indicated which direction Dewey had been traveling when he left them, east or west. So far, all the clues had pointed west, which meant Dewey had yet to return through any of the towns they had traveled through to that point. There was no way Clive could prove that part, but so far Amber's level of accuracy had been uncanny, so for the time being at least, he was stuck with her. He assumed there had to be some sort of pattern to the clues, but despite his constant badgering, Amber wouldn't reveal what the pattern was, no doubt because she realized the minute Clive figured it out, he would ditch her faster than she could devour a Big Turk candy bar, and that was saying something.

Clive glanced at Amber as they passed a sign that indicated yet another miniscule town was just ahead. "Well, what are we looking for this time?"

She looked out the window. Perhaps as part of a coordinated marketing effort to increase tourism, each small town across the prairies had its own roadside attraction. Some went the route of "big," featuring the world's biggest tomahawk, turtle, teepee, tiger lily, coffee pot, oil can, machine gun, moose, frog, bull, or whooping crane. Others went "small," including miniature versions of grain elevators, a barn, an opera house, and the Eiffel Tower. Still others went for the bizarre, featuring objects that, on the surface at least, had nothing to do with rural Saskatchewan, including a camel made out of automobile parts, a missile, a sasquatch, a giant zombie hand coming out of the ground, and life-size replicas of the vehicles from The Flintstones. This town had gone for "big" and "tall," featuring what it claimed to be the world's largest swather, situated at the top of a fifty-foot pole.

"First things first," Amber said, her eyes going from the swather to an upcoming service station.

"Are you serious?" Clive said. "You have to go again?"

Amber glared at him. "Do you want my help or not?"

Clive sighed and then signaled to turn in to the service station.

As Amber went inside to do her thing, Clive waited impatiently in the car, drumming his fingers on the steering wheel. These bathroom breaks alone were driving him around the bend. He was beginning to think her bladder was the size of a walnut or maybe even smaller. What kind of person had to stop every—

His train of thought came to a sudden halt as his eyes shot to the service station door. The bathroom breaks, always at a service station and never at a restaurant. Amber insisted on it. And often at a certain kind of service station. Could there be a connection between her frequent pit stops and the clues? What was she doing in there besides going to the bathroom and buying copious amounts of junk food? Was she in cahoots with Dewey? Was she calling him on the phone and leading Clive on some sort of wild goose chase?

Just as Clive was about to go inside to check on her, Amber came out, laden with yet another load of snacks, none of which she ever offered to share with him. Not only did her body's ability to metabolize so much garbage amaze him, so did her ability to afford it. She must have burned through a couple hundred dollars so far in the short time he had known her.

"Feeling better now?" he asked as she piled into the car, some of her treasures tumbling into Clive's lap as she kicked aside mounds of trash on the floor to make room for her feet.

"No, I'm not feeling better," she said, giving him a sharp look as she tore a package of Twizzlers open with her teeth. "I'm still stuck in this car with you, aren't I?"

Clive raised his left eyebrow. "You're stuck in this car with me?"

Amber rolled her eyes, not wanting to go around the same mulberry bush again. "Do you want me to do my thing or not?"

Clive nodded. "Go for it."

Munching noisily on two Twizzlers, she closed her eyes and put her left palm to her forehead. "What would Dewey do?" she said and then immediately opened her eyes. "Check the swather."

"The what?" Clive asked, gazing at her in confusion.

She jabbed her thumb over her shoulder. "The big harvester thingy on the top of the pole that we passed on the way into town."

Clive continued to stare at her. She had been so quick about it, as if she already knew the answer even before she closed her eyes. "Are you sure?"

She glared at him with contempt. "Of course I'm sure. I haven't been wrong yet, have I?"

"What are we supposed to find there?"

"A tongue print."

"A what?"

Amber swallowed her mouthful of Twizzlers and then yanked at her seatbelt to put it on, pulling so hard that it locked, which only angered her further and caused her to yank even harder, causing the seatbelt to remain locked, which frustrated her even more. "Can we just hit the road already? I'll show you when we get there."

Clive gave her one final look and then put the car in drive and cranked a U-turn. He would get to the bottom of Amber's "psychic abilities" one way or another. And if he discovered she was lying to him in some way . . .

§

Mrs. Muller was ironing in front of the TV while watching one of her favorite daytime soap operas, All My Children, a guilty pleasure that not even her husband, Dennis, knew about. She was so enraptured by the show that she had stopped ironing altogether, holding the iron in place over the dress she had been preparing for a date night with Dennis as she waited to see how "Tad the Cad" would react when he discovered his marriage to Dottie was based on a lie. Just as the big event was about to unfold, the doorbell rang.

Mrs. Muller growled in frustration as she looked over her shoulder toward the door. "Not now!" she hissed and then turned back to the screen. "Come on, come on already," she said, urging the actors to move faster through the scene. "Just get it over with."

The doorbell rang again.

"I'm coming!" she shouted, unable to keep the frustration from her voice. Just then she smelled something. She sniffed again. If she didn't know better, she would have thought something was—

"Burning! My dress is burning!" She removed the iron from where she had parked it on the dress, revealing an iron-shaped black spot. "No! It's ruined!" She held it up, and the burnt part of the fabric fell away, revealing Dottie's frightened face on the TV. Then the show cut to commercial. "No, wait, what did she say? I missed it! What was her big secret?"

The doorbell rang again. She turned toward the door clutching the smoking dress in her fist, her teeth clenched. "Whoever it is, it darn well better be worth it!"

She stomped through the kitchen and whipped open the front door, revealing Chad and Andrew standing on her front porch. Both of them were smiling, which was a rare occurrence for Andrew, who almost always had a serious look on his face as his brain worked overtime to solve one scientific problem or another.

"Good afternoon, Mrs. Muller," Chad said brightly.

"What's good about it?" she snapped, still ticked about her dress and missing out on Dottie's big reveal.

"Well, it's sunny for starters," Chad said, still smiling, "and it's not too—" He stopped and sniffed. "Did you leave something on the stove, Mrs. Muller? I could swear I smell something burn—"

"No, I did not leave something on the stove," Mrs. Muller said, hiding the burnt dress behind her back. "Now what do you two jokers want?" She craned her neck to look past them. "And where's the third stooge?"

Chad glanced at Andrew, both of their smiles fading as they went into their prepared act. "You mean Matt?"

"I said 'stooge,' didn't I?" Mrs. Muller said, tapping her foot. "And make it snappy. You're cooling off the entire house."

"Uh, right," Chad said. "Could we actually come inside for a minute?"

Mrs. Muller gazed longingly over her shoulder toward the TV and then turned back to the boys, grimacing in resignation as she opened the door wider to let them in. There was no point going back to the show now. She'd just have to read a summary of the episode in the following week's issue of Soap Opera Digest, which she bought every week on the sly.

Once the boys were inside and she had closed the door, Chad resumed his explanation. "Matt is sick."

"Oh yeah?" Mrs. Muller said. "In the head? We already knew that."

"Actually, the doctor thinks it might be pneumonia," Andrew replied, his face serious to help communicate the gravity of the situation.

"Which one?" Mrs. Muller asked. Andrew looked at Chad. Neither of them had anticipated that question.

"I-I'm not sure," Andrew admitted. "I didn't know there were different types of pneumonia, but I'm sure there—"

"No, no," Mrs. Muller replied. "Which doctor?" She wasn't too fond of either Dr. Maharaj, but she definitely preferred one over the other. She just wasn't sure which one. However, she did know one thing: whichever doctor would deign to treat Matt Taylor was definitely not the physician she wanted caring for her medical needs.

Andrew looked at Chad to answer, seeing as Matt was Chad's brother and would know best who their family doctor was. "Uh, I'm not sure, Mrs. Muller," Chad said.

"You don't even know your own doctor's name?" Mrs. Muller asked, realizing immediately she was in the same position.

Chad shook his head. "No. I hardly ever go to the doctor. Anyway, Matt's pretty sick, so he has to stay at home in bed right now. Anyway, we were wondering if—"

"Dean isn't here, if that's what you want to know. He's at school working on his snow sculpture, or so he says. If I didn't know better, I'd say he wasn't sculpting anything. He's just trying to get out of doing his chores."

"Actually, Mrs. Muller," Chad said, glancing warily at Andrew as he prepared to take the plunge. "We didn't come here to talk to Dean. We came here to talk to you."

She eyed them warily. "You want to talk to me?"

Chad swallowed hard and then nodded. "Yes."

"Then be my guest," Mrs. Muller said, gesturing for them to sit at the kitchen table. "I could use a good laugh. Just one minute." She hurried into the living room and turned off the TV. Thankfully, it was still on commercial, so the boys had no idea what she had been watching. Then she returned to the kitchen, opened the cupboard under the kitchen sink, and whipped the dress into the trash. She had bought it on a great sale at K-mart, so it wasn't that much of a loss. She sat down across from the boys at the kitchen table, took a second to compose herself, then laced her fingers together and rested her chin on her hands as she pasted a sickly sweet smile onto her face. "Now . . . what did you want to talk about?"

Andrew and Chad both swallowed hard as they exchanged a frightened look. This was going to be a lot tougher than they thought.

14

The Dig Begins

Looking for a way to distract himself from his dinner date dilemma, Staff Sergeant Romanowski decided to go out on patrol. Not only would it help clear his head, while he was at it, he could pass by both doctors' homes in the hope that something would jog his brain about which one had issued the dinner invitation. He realized he was probably being ridiculous and that he should simply go to the hospital, confess his confusion to Bash and Harpreet, and clear things up right away. While that would get him out of the ticklish situation with Nurse Chaykowski, it would also diminish his reputation as an investigator extraordinaire, especially if word of his confusion got around, and he definitely could not have that. If he was going to get out of this tough spot, he would have to do it on his own.

As he emerged from his office, he found constables Chambers and Rogers sitting at their desks on opposite sides of the room tossing a mini football back and forth, both of them trying to make it just scrape the suspended ceiling tiles before it arced down into the receiver's hands.

"Yo, Chief, check this out," Rogers said. "The world's best no-look pass." He closed his eyes and then tossed the football to Chambers, a perfect spiral that just nudged a water-stained ceiling tile before it curved down right into Chambers' outstretched hands. Rogers opened his eyes and grinned at the staff sergeant. "Not too shabby, huh?"

Romanowski pursed his lips, divots forming in his cheeks as his mustache bristled. "Don't you two have anything more productive to do? Some paperwork to fill out? Crimes to solve? When was the last time either of you was out on patrol?"

"Crimes? In this town?" Chambers said, the thickness of his mustache rivaling Romanowski's soup strainer. "You're kidding, right? After all, it's too cold for anyone to be scaling the grain elevators, right? Besides, it's Sunday. This town is always quiet on Sundays." He whipped a bullet pass at Rogers, who reached up and caught it with one hand. "Nice snag," Chambers said, smiling.

Both constables jumped as Romanowski pounded the desk beside him with his fist. "Do I need to remind you two that you are officers of the law, funded by the taxpayers of this fine country to serve and protect the public trust?"

"No, sir!" Chambers and Rogers replied in unison, snapping to attention in their seats.

"Good. Need I also remind you that we recently had a potential car thief right here in this very town who is currently at large?"

"No, sir," Rogers and Chambers replied.

"Just one question, sir," Chambers said.

Romanowski took a deep breath and then heaved it out. "Yes?"

"Isn't that your case, sir?"

"And aren't you the one who lost track of him?" Rogers added.

Romanowski glowered at his underlings, realizing they

were right but not wanting to admit it. "Just put that football away and get to work. This is the RCMP, not the CFL," he said, emphasizing the letter of each abbreviation.

With that, Romanowski stomped out, reminded that he had two mysteries to solve: the dinner date and Dewey's disappearance. In both cases, his reputation as a police officer of distinction was on the line.

The more he thought about it, the more he realized Dewey was at the heart of all his problems. If Dewey hadn't gotten into that car accident, he wouldn't have been in the hospital, and Romanowski wouldn't have had to go there to question him, which meant Dr. Maharaj wouldn't have issued the dinner invitation, and Nurse Chaykowski wouldn't have finagled her way into it as Romanowski's date, and he wouldn't have had to lie to Henrietta. As he stepped out into the brisk morning air, he was more determined than ever to track down the little lawbreaker. And if Dewey was guilty of even half of what Romanowski suspected him of, he was going to throw the book at him.

§

Mrs. Taylor looked up from adding ingredients to a Mixmaster as Chad tramped through the kitchen toward his and Matt's bedroom wearing his snow gear and snowmobile helmet, his tinted face shield concealing his features.

"What have I told you boys about wearing your snow boots in the house?" she asked, scrutinizing the paisley-patterned linoleum floor for wet marks.

Chad said something to her in reply that she couldn't quite make out.

"What was that?"

"I said my boots are dry!" Chad called from the bedroom.

"They could still leave black marks on the floor!" Mrs. Taylor said.

"OK. Sorry, Mom," Chad replied. "I won't do it again. I just forgot something and didn't want to take them off. I'm already late."

In the boys' bedroom, "Chad" raised his face shield, revealing he was actually Matt. "Whew, that was a close one," Matt whispered. "Thanks for covering for me."

"No problem," Chad replied, having just responded to their mom on Matt's behalf. He lay back down and pulled the covers up to his chin. Matt and Chad's hair wasn't quite the same color, so Chad was also sporting a toque. Between the cap and the covers, they hoped that in the darkened room, their parents wouldn't be able to tell the difference. "But I still don't know what I'm going to do for the next few hours lying here in your bed like this."

Although Matt wasn't officially allowed to be involved in the dig, seeing as the snow maze was his brainchild, Chad had agreed to let him take the first shift, so the project could get off on the right foot. Wearing the snowmobile helmet in the house had been Matt's idea, an easy way for him to sneak out right under their parents' noses, especially considering the boys had matching jackets and snow pants. Thankfully, the boys were almost the same size, so the minor difference in height wouldn't give him away.

"You can read under the covers. Here's a flashlight." Matt reached over and grabbed a flashlight and some Archie comic books off his desk, tossing them onto the bed.

"It gets too hot after a few minutes. Besides, what if Mom comes in to give me medicine or check my temperature, and I don't have time to turn it off? She's going to wonder what's up. The only way this can work is if I pretend I'm asleep. Otherwise, if she talks to me, my voice will give me away."

Matt shrugged. "I'm sure you'll come up with something. Maybe you can actually go to sleep."

"And risk the covers coming off my face? No way. Besides, I still don't know how you're going to get away with coming back home. It's not like you can wear your snow gear and helmet into the bedroom again. Mom and Dad will know something's up for sure."

"That's why you told them you wouldn't be home until late, remember? I'll come back once everyone is in bed. I'll park the snowmobile at the end of the driveway and then walk into the yard to make sure all the lights are off. Then I'll come inside. If Mom and Dad ask why you didn't drive into the yard, tell them you were worried the sound of the snowmobile would wake everyone up."

Chad couldn't argue with that. As usual, Matt had thought through every detail, although Chad worried his younger brother was getting way too good at this deception thing.

"All right," he said, rolling over to face the wall. "Have fun. You know I won't be having any."

"I will. And look on the bright side. You're getting out of a ton of work, and when you show up for your shift, lots of the snow maze should already be done."

"That doesn't make me feel any better," Chad replied. "I enjoy digging snow tunnels, you know."

"Well, remember, it was your idea to build this thing on Mrs. Muller's land, and it was your idea for me to play sick," Matt said, knowing Chad couldn't argue with that. "Catch you on the flippity flip." He pulled his face shield back down and went out.

"What time do you expect to be back?" Mrs. Taylor asked as Matt passed back through the kitchen. Once again, he replied with something she didn't understand. Before she could ask him to repeat himself, he was out the door. She shook her head as she flattened some pie dough with a rolling pin. "That boy really needs to learn how to enunciate!"

§

As Dean walked down the street toward his house at around noon, he couldn't have been happier. It didn't hurt that the sky was clear, and the sun was glistening off the hoarfrost that coated the otherwise bare elm trees that arced over the sidewalk, creating a perfect winter wonderland display. What really had his heart singing though wasn't the weather but his snow sculpture. Not only had Joy been away that morning, which meant he had been able to avoid her constant pestering and hints that she still didn't have a date for the dance, his sculpture was coming along beautifully. If everything went according to plan, there was no way Joyce could refuse his invitation to the dance after seeing it. His only concern was that someone else had already asked her out. However, seeing as Joyce thought most boys her age were stupid and immature, it was highly unlikely she would have said yes. It didn't occur to him that, being two years younger than Joyce, she probably put Dean in the same category—or worse. After all, in his mind, they had already shared their first kiss. The fact that it had happened when he had ambushed her during the live broadcast of their radio show the previous spring didn't diminish its significance one bit in his mind. The way Dean saw it, Joyce was as good as his.

As he veritably skipped up his front steps, he paused, his hand on the screen door as he spied a pile of equipment that looked like it had been recently placed on the wraparound porch to his right. It included all manner of shovels, bundles of rope, a pickaxe, buckets, and . . . a snorkel? Dean picked up the snorkel and looked at it. Had his mother been cleaning out the shed or—

Before he could complete that thought, Mrs. Muller opened the door, her arms laden with more equipment, including tarps, a headlamp, tree-pruning shears, and a hand saw. She peeked around the pile of junk at Dean. "Oh good, you're home! I was just going to come down and get you." She dumped the gear onto the pile and then dusted off her hands. "You haul this stuff to the van, and I'll get the rest of it from downstairs. No time to waste!"

"Wait, what the heck is going on?" Dean asked as she turned to go back inside. "Where are you taking all this stuff? The thrift store?"

"The question is, where are you taking all this stuff?" Mrs. Muller said, thumping him in the chest as she grinned at him.

"Me? What—"

"Are you hungry?" Mrs. Muller asked.

"Yes, in fact I was just going to—"

"Good. I packed a lunch for you." She shoved a bulging brown paper bag into his arms, along with a thermos. "There's homemade chicken noodle soup in there. It should stay warm for hours, and you'll be thankful for it by then."

"By when?"

"When it gets too dark to dig. But then again, Andrew said there's going to be a full moon tonight with no clouds, and the temperature's only going to be a bit below freezing, so, technically speaking, you could keep going all night if you didn't have school tomorrow. At any rate, if you get tired, you can always take a nap." She handed him a sleeping bag to emphasize her point.

"Hold on a second," Dean said as his mother continued to pile more gear into his arms. "What are you talking about? Dig what? I'm not doing any digging. I was just coming home for a snack and then heading back to work on my snow sculpture."

"Not anymore you're not."

"But I have to! The Valentine's Day dance is on Tuesday night, and I—"

"Since when do you dance? Besides, you can sculpt on your own time. Right now we have bigger fish to fry. Now grab this gear and get moving." She picked up a load and shoved it into Dean's arms, then spun him toward the car and pushed him forward.

Dean stumbled down the steps and then turned back to look at her, barely holding onto all the gear. "Fish? What are you talking about? What fish?"

Mrs. Muller leered down at him from the porch. "The biggest fish of all . . . Matt Taylor. I'm about to skin him, gut him, and fry him for dinner, and you're going to help."

15

A Strange Apparition

Dewey was elated. After Zee took him to the scene of the accident—all that remained of the moose was a bloody smear on the highway, so Zee missed out on his steaks—it was a simple matter to figure out which gravel road he had driven down to bury the hard-shell case. The only problem was, the site was nearly three kilometers out of town, and he had no way to get back out there. He couldn't ask Zee to drive him because then he'd have to explain what was going on. Even if Zee agreed to keep his secret, there was no way Earl would cut him in on the deal. In fact, telling Zee could endanger both of their lives. Dewey considered trying to steal a car, seeing as most people tended to leave their vehicles running and unlocked as they dashed inside the post office to get their mail, but in such a small town, he was almost certain to be discovered. Therefore, Dewey's only choice was to wait until dark and then travel there on foot. The moon would be full again, so visibility wouldn't be an issue. However, it would increase the possibility of him being seen. He just hoped the local RCMP ended their highway patrol early.

His heart pounding in anticipation, it took all of Dewey's patience to wait for the sun to set. He killed some time by grabbing a meal at the local Chinese food restaurant, spending most of what remained of his meager supply of cash. However, now that he was this close to getting the case, money was no object. If everything went according to plan, soon he'd have more money than he'd ever dreamed possible—or at least Earl would. However, even if Earl gave Dewey only a small percentage of what he made off the deal, it would be more money than Dewey had ever seen before.

By the time Dewey finished his last egg roll, the sun had gone down. Wanting to be sure the coast was clear, he decided to stake out the police station, hiding in some bushes across the street. Once all three patrol cars were accounted for, he hurried toward the highway, eager for his ordeal to finally be over, though he did take time to buy a coffee at a service station to ensure he could stay awake.

The moon was exceptionally bright, so bright that not only did he still have to wear his sunglasses, he also had to use his umbrella to shield himself from its white glow. Even then it was just enough to prevent a throbbing headache. He knew he cut a strange figure as he walked down the highway like that, so whenever a vehicle passed, he laid down in the ditch until the vehicle roared past. Thankfully, there wasn't much traffic that evening. The sky was clear, which made it cold, but Dewey had a fire burning inside that no amount of cold weather could snuff out.

§

A bobbing yellow light illuminated the entrance to a tunnel at the snow maze building site. Moments later, Dean wriggled out of the tunnel with his arms crossed, pushing a mound of snow in front of him. After shoveling it away from the entrance and down the hill, he sat up and turned off his headlamp, scanning the sky above. Even though the moon was full, millions of stars were still visible, creating a stunning display, especially considering they were far away from all other forms of light pollution. As he surveyed the landscape though, he shivered. Not from cold—digging snow tunnels was hot, sweaty work—but due to the eerie shadows that the moonlight created, transforming barren trees into wraithlike figures and leftover round bales into hulking monstrosities. It was the perfect setting for the type of gothic horror movies that Dean had been staying up late to watch on TV lately, though now he regretted those decisions.

Hearing something behind him in the tunnel, Dean moved out of the way. Seconds later, Andrew emerged, also pushing a mound of snow in front of him. After depositing it down the hill, he turned off his headlamp and sat next to Dean.

"I think it's time to dig an emergency exit," Andrew said, huffing from exertion. "This run is getting way too long to push all this snow. We'll never get finished at this rate."

Before Dean could reply, they heard something a short distance away on the slope they were excavating. It was "Chad," or so it appeared to Dean.

"I still don't understand why he's wearing his snowmobile helmet," Dean said as they watched "Chad's" headlamp bob around. He had duct-taped it to the top of his helmet.

"He's . . . he's just being safety conscious," Andrew said, scrambling to cover for Matt. "In fact, we should probably all be wearing helmets." Considering Matt's recent run-in with Dean, he and the other boys had agreed it was best to keep Matt's involvement in the project a secret from Dean as well in case he accidentally spilled the beans to his mother—or did so deliberately out of spite. Keeping Matt apart from Dean and having Matt wear the snowmobile helmet was the simplest way to do it.

Dean gave Andrew a cockeyed look. "Helmets? Snow is soft, remember?" He picked some up and dropped it on his head to demonstrate. "It's not like we're in danger of getting a concussion even if the roof does collapse, which it won't."

"No, but a helmet . . ." Andrew paused, his mind racing for a response. "In the event of a collapse, one of the biggest concerns is suffocating under the snow. A helmet can provide an air pocket that will buy you a bit more time to dig your way out."

Dean looked at Andrew in horror. "Why didn't you tell me that earlier? My mom sent me with all sorts of safety equipment, and you didn't think to tell me to bring a helmet?"

Andrew's eyes searched the night sky for an answer. "I . . . I never thought about it until just now." And in truth, he hadn't.

"Well, that does it. From now on, helmets should be mandatory. I'm definitely wearing one the next time I come, and you should too. In fact, I insist."

Andrew shrugged, kicking himself for having suggested the idea. "I guess so."

"Speaking of which," Dean said, "I won't be able to come right away after school tomorrow. I need to work on my snow sculpture."

"That's fine," Andrew said. "I'm just glad you're willing to help at all. There's no way Chad and I can dig this entire thing on our own." He pulled out Matt's hand-drawn map and consulted it. "This thing is huge. In fact, I don't know how we're going to get it all done in time even with your help." The boys were planning to complete the snow maze in time to announce it at the unveiling of the snow sculptures that Tuesday morning, so kids could come out and go through it following the Valentine's Day dance. However, Andrew was a bit concerned about the forecast. It was calling for temperatures to rise to close to zero over the next few days, which was good in terms of digging, but it also created the potential for a blizzard, which would be bad for business if it made driving precarious.

"Well, normally I wouldn't care, but with the way Matt's been treating me lately, I agree with my mom. This is the best way to get back at him: to build his dream snow maze but Matt not be able to participate. How's he doing by the way? I hear he's pretty sick."

"You should call him," Andrew said, turning on his headlamp and heading back into the tunnel. "You two really need to bury the hatchet. You're too good of friends to keep carrying on like this."

"I know," Dean replied. "And we will. I just want to enjoy finally having one up on him for a little longer. Speaking of which—"

Dean froze, his gloved finger on the switch of his headlamp, which he had yet to turn on. He blinked as he stared at the darkened field, unable to believe his eyes. Then he turned on his headlamp, shining it across the field and trying to verify if what he had seen was real or just his imagination, but the light was too weak to reach the spot where the apparition had appeared. He turned his headlamp off and waited for his eyes to readjust to the darkness, but when they did, nothing was there. A cold chill crept down his spine.

Without a second to lose, he turned and dove back

into the tunnel, scrambling along on his hands and knees. "Andrew! Andrew!"

Just down the road from the snow maze site, Dewey peeked out from his hiding spot behind a gnarled poplar tree. He was just able to make out the black dots of the snow tunnel entrances in the moonlight, but whoever was digging them had disappeared back inside. He exhaled with relief. Perhaps he hadn't been spotted after all. Then his body tensed with anxiety. Someone was digging in the exact spot where he had buried the case! Who were they, and how had they found out about it? He hadn't told anyone—heck, even he hadn't been able to remember where the spot was until earlier that day. Could he have said something in his delirium prior to waking up from his concussion? Had Zee figured it out somehow? If so, why weren't they digging along the barbed-wire fence? Maybe what he said had been vague, and they had tried digging in other spots before this one, not knowing that all they had to do was search for the padlock, and they would find the case.

Dewey had no idea what was going on, but he was certain of one thing: getting the case was no longer a cakewalk; it was a race. He simply had to get it before they did. His life depended on it. But considering there were three of them and only one of him, he decided it was best to get out of there while he still could and return in the morning. He just hoped he wouldn't be too late.

§

Early in the morning, while it was still dark and cold, Clive carefully opened his motel room door, not wanting to wake Amber, who was staying next to him. She had insisted on separate rooms to make sure there was no "funny business," as she called it. Despite the cost of the extra room, Clive was only too happy to pay it. Anything to get a few hours of peace and quiet away from Amber. That's exactly what he was looking for right now, peace and quiet as he ate breakfast and perhaps read the newspaper. That and a chance to avoid paying for Amber's meal. When it came to junk food, she seemed to have unlimited funds, but when it came to more expensive items, like motel rooms and meals, it seemed as if her cash flow suddenly dried up, and Clive had to foot the bill for everything. Considering her so-called psychic ability to track Dewey's movements—about which Clive was still skeptical—he supposed it was a fair exchange. However, he was confident they were closing in on their prey, and it was only a matter of time before he could—

"Going somewhere?"

Clive nearly jumped out of his skin as he spun around to find Amber silhouetted by the glow of a soft drink vending machine behind him.

"How long have you been standing there?" he asked, shivering from the shock and the sub-zero temperature.

"Long enough." He heard her pop the tab on a soda can and watched as she tilted it back and took a slug.

"Pepsi? For breakfast?" Clive said, catching a glint of the can's label in the light of the drink machine. "Your dentist must love you."

She lowered the can and wiped her lips with the back of her hand. "I haven't been to a dentist in years." She paused and burped. "Now, what's to eat?"

Clive sighed, the placid vision of him combing through the travel section of the newspaper and planning his getaway while sipping coffee and orange juice and eating two eggs, two strips of bacon, hash browns, and rye toast smothered in butter and jam dissipating from his mind. "I was thinking about Humpty's," he said weakly, knowing it was never going to happen now.

Amber scoffed. "Humpty's? Are you kidding me? What a waste of time. We're going to 7-Eleven."

"Excuse me?"

"They have the best breakfast sandwiches."

He gave her a blank stare. "They do?"

"The name Jimmy Dean mean anything to you?" she said, stepping forward.

"No, I—"

"They make a savory breakfast croissant, a spicy sausage bagel, an Italian breakfast panini, and my favorite—a sausage-and-waffle breakfast stack. All you gotta do is take it out of the bag, pop it in the microwave, and voila. Top it off with a donut or a Twinkie and some coffee—I take mine with four cubes of sugar and two dollops of cream, but you already know that—and you've got the breakfast of champions. In fact, if you throw the donut or Twinkie in the microwave for a few seconds too, it totally elevates the meal."

Clive continued staring at her, as if observing a previously undiscovered life form. "The microwave? You put your entire breakfast in the microwave? At 7-Eleven?"

"Yup. Coffee too because they never make it hot enough. In fact, you know what, Jeeves-y old boy?" She put her arm around him. He looked down at her hand on his shoulder in alarm. "I'm feeling so good this morning that breakfast is my treat. I'm going to shake you out of your stuffy British attitude one way or another."

§

"I swear that's what I saw," Dean said later that night as all four boys convened on their walkie-talkies for an update. "A man was standing on the road wearing a hat and holding an umbrella, and he was staring right at us!"

Earlier in the call, Dean and Matt had reconciled their differences over Matt's misunderstanding about Dean supposedly sabotaging their previous snow maze building site. However, neither Matt nor the other boys had revealed to Dean that Matt was merely faking his illness and that it had been him and not Chad who had been digging with them. Even though Dean no longer held a grudge against Matt, they were still worried he would be unable to keep the secret from his mom, especially once he discovered they had deceived him about Matt.

"That doesn't make any sense," Matt said. "Who walks around late at night in the middle of nowhere in February with an umbrella?"

"You'd just been digging pretty hard, you were tired, and maybe the oxygen level in those tunnels is lower than normal," Andrew said. "It could have been a hallucination."

"Oxygen level?" Dean blurted. "No one said anything about low oxygen levels in the snow tunnels. If my mom finds out—"

"It's just a theory," Andrew said quickly. "It was a stupid idea. I'm sure the oxygen levels in the tunnels are just fine. In fact, my dad has an air quality monitor at home that he uses in the chicken barn that I can borrow to test it."

Dean relaxed somewhat at the mention of that. "OK, but if I wasn't hallucinating, that means some strange dude really was out there late last night watching us dig.

What kind of a person would do that?"

None of the other boys had an answer, but all of them felt creeped out by the possibility.

16

Busted

Staff Sergeant Romanowski pounded the steering wheel of his police cruiser in frustration as it sat idling in the darkness early on Monday morning at the north end of Main Street following a long overnight shift. In a community of just 1,300 people, why was he having such a difficult time tracking down Dewey Biggs? After all, the doctors reported that Dewey had left the hospital wearing sunglasses, a rumpled hat, and carrying an umbrella—in February, no less—so how much more conspicuous could he be?

Romanowski had patrolled the town several times, checked back in at the hospital—careful to avoid Nurse Chaykowski when he did—and queried the owners of various local establishments where Dewey might have gone, including the motel, the pool hall, the grocery store, and the pub. The last sighting of him was at the Chinese food restaurant the previous evening, but after that, the trail had gone cold. Dewey must have stayed overnight somewhere—it was too cold to stay outside. That left only two possibilities. One, he had a local collaborator who was helping him—or some naïve individual had taken him in out of pity—or two, Dewey had defied Romanowski's order not to leave town.

If that were the case, Romanowski would put out a province-wide alert, and when they found the little reprobate, he would throw the book at him. However, still wanting to give Dewey the benefit of the doubt, Romanowski put his cruiser in drive and decided to patrol the town one last time. But first things first. He needed a coffee.

§

Dewey was stiff and sore from having spent a few hours sleeping on the floor of Zee's Towing. While there the previous day, he had unlatched the window over the toilet in Zee's bathroom on the off chance that he needed a place to stay or bug out if the heat came down on him, and he was glad he had. Not wanting to draw attention to himself by showing up at the hospital late at night or face resistance when he insisted on leaving again early the next morning, Zee's office made the perfect hideaway. Dewey hadn't counted on Sarge being there—Zee kept him in the office overnight in lieu of a security system—but after the dog's initial shock of seeing Dewey emerge from the bathroom, Sarge seemed quite happy to have an overnight companion, and he snuggled in next to Dewey on the floor, keeping him warm.

Despite his exhaustion, the warmth, and the unexpected company, Dewey had a hard time sleeping. He kept waking himself up throughout the night to check the time. Not only did he want to be well away from the office before Zee showed up, he also wanted to get to the dig site as soon as possible. He figured if they had been working late, they would likely sleep in, which meant early morning would be his best time to get back there and grab the case. He just hoped they hadn't pulled an all-nighter and that he wouldn't encounter a second shift when he showed up.

His eyes bleary with sleep, Dewey slipped out the window, landing in a heap in the snowbank that had built up against the back of the building. Somewhat wobbly on his feet due to the concussion and exhaustion, he got up, dusted himself off, and headed across the darkened town. As he walked, he found some change in his pocket and figured he had just enough left to buy a coffee at the service station on the way out of town, and boy, did he ever need it.

§

Clive still wasn't sure how he had managed to convince Amber to wake up in the dark for the second morning in a row and hit the road prior to sunrise. Perhaps it was the promise of a free Jimmy Dean microwave-infused breakfast, or maybe she was getting just as sick of the search as he was. Whatever the case, she was in the passenger seat now, sound asleep, as the New Yorker cruised down the highway. Not only was the silence blissful, as Clive examined her, he realized that when she wasn't singing off-key, hurling insults at him, complaining, or cramming her face full of junk food, she wasn't all that bad looking. In fact, under different circumstances, he might even have called her pretty, which made her partnership with Dewey, as brief as it was, all the more surprising.

Thinking he was getting delusional due to lack of sleep, Clive quickly looked away and gave his head a shake. When they passed a sign indicating the next town was just one mile ahead, he was glad for the excuse to pull in and grab a coffee. After glancing at the fuel gauge, he realized they needed gas too. He just hoped the service station sold Jimmy Dean breakfast sandwiches—which weren't as awful as he thought they'd be initially—or he shuddered to think how Amber would react.

§

Dewey was huddled over the coffee machine in the service station ladling spoonfuls of powdered coffee creamer into his extra-large Styrofoam cup when he heard giggling at the front counter. He looked up and saw the teenage gas jockey and the cashier grinning at him.

"What are you, a male version of Mary Poppins or something?" the gas jockey asked. He was a good-looking Aboriginal kid with a broad face and long dark hair pulled back into a ponytail. He was wearing a snowsuit and a bright orange hunter's cap with earflaps that hung down. His companion was also Aboriginal, a teenage girl who looked like she could be his sister.

Dewey looked at them in confusion and then glanced at his umbrella and finally made the connection. He held it up, along with a packet of sugar. "What can I say? A spoonful of sugar makes the medicine go down."

The cashier leaned over the counter and whispered something to the gas jockey, which made him smile even broader. "She wants you to sing that song. Come on, Mary Poppins man, sing!"

Dewey was about to open his mouth to protest that he had a horrible singing voice when they heard a dinging sound as a car pulled up to the pumps.

"Guess it'll have to wait," the gas jockey said, putting on a pair of long beaded leather mitts. "Oh, look, it's the fuzz!"

Dewey looked out the front window, nearly dropping the sugar packet into his coffee as he caught sight of the red-and-blue lights on the vehicle's roof. Not the police!

Not now! Not when he was so close! Leaving his coffee, he raced up to the counter, ducking behind a display of potato chips to conceal his face from the front window.

"I need the key to your restroom. Now!"

The cashier looked up at him, pulled away from reading the latest issue of The National Enquirer. "What's your hurry?"

"I just need it!"

She nodded sagely. "Coffee has that effect on you too, huh?" She reached behind the counter and withdrew a two-foot-long section of hockey stick with a key chained to it. Dewey snatched it and then raced toward the back of the store, suddenly stopping and looking around. He turned back at the cashier. "Where is it?"

"Where's what?"

"The bathroom!" Dewey cried, well beyond the limit of his patience.

She pointed to the front door. "You have to go outside. It's along the side of the building."

"The front door? Why didn't you tell me that in the first place?"

The cashier shrugged. "You didn't ask."

"Does this place have a rear exit?"

She nodded once again. "Yup. It's in the back."

No kidding, Dewey thought. "Can I use it to get to the bathroom?"

She glanced outside and then looked him up and down. "You don't like the police either, huh?"

"Let's just say I'd like to give the police officer out there a spoonful of sugar," Dewey replied, "right in his gas tank." She nodded in understanding, returning her attention to her reading. "You can use it."

Clenching his teeth in an attempt to dull the pain in

his throbbing head, Dewey raced for the back door just as the bell dinged, indicating another car had pulled up to the pumps.

§

"I don't see any Jimmy Deans. You told me there would be Jimmy Deans!" Amber complained a few minutes later as she and Clive combed through the service station's meager refrigerated food section. "And if I have to wait much longer to go to the bathroom, I'm going to burst!"

"How about one of these?" Clive asked, pulling a packaged sausage-and-egg sandwich out of the cooler. "It looks pretty good."

"Jimmy Jones? Are you kidding me?" Amber said, grabbing it and throwing it back into the cooler. "Total rip-off."

"Keep it down," Clive hissed, eyeing the RCMP officer who was leaning on the front counter as he waited for the gas jockey to finish filling his cruiser.

"Why don't you go ask him if he's seen Dewey?" Amber whispered. "That's what you do in every other town."

"I don't know," Clive said, pretending to sift through a rack of packaged nuts as he snuck a look at the officer. "I don't like the look of him."

"Well, if you won't, I will," Amber said. "I just want to get this over with." She started toward the till, but Clive grabbed her arm and pulled her close.

"Since when do you need a police officer to help you find Dewey?" he hissed. "What about your psychic abilities? Why don't you just do your 'What would Dewey do?' thing right here, right now?"

Amber glanced at a circular display rack of roadmaps

near the front door and then turned back to Clive. "Not with you here."

"Why not?"

"It's too hard to concentrate."

"You've done it with me around before."

"Well, I can't do it now. I'm too angry. And I have to use the bathroom."

"Fine," Clive said, releasing her arm as the police officer, who boasted a truly impressive mustache, looked over at them. "I'll wait in the car. As for breakfast, I'm withdrawing my offer. You're on your own for that too."

"Fine," Amber said, pulling away from him.

§

Dewey waited in the bathroom until he heard a car drive away. He opened the door a crack and peeked out. The police cruiser was gone. All that remained at the pumps was a white Chrysler New Yorker. His heart rate slowing somewhat, Dewey opened the door all the way.

"Finally!" a woman's voice said from behind him, nearly causing Dewey to leap out of his skin. As he turned to face her, he realized there was something familiar about that voice. In fact, if he didn't know better, he would have sworn it was . . .

Amber! His ex-girlfriend. Standing right in front of him, her hand extended angrily, demanding the key.

"You better not have left the seat up!"

In a daze, he held out the piece of hockey stick with the key attached, and she snatched it from him. As shocked as Dewey was to encounter her in the middle of nowhere, he was also confused. Why didn't she recognize him? Then he realized: the hat, the sunglasses, and the—

"Nice umbrella, loser," she said, slamming the door behind her.

Not wanting to be there when she came out in case she finally saw through his getup, he hurried toward the front door of the service station, determined to grab his coffee and get out of there. But just as he reached for the door handle, he looked inside and saw another familiar face.

Clive!

He was combing through a rack of roadmaps as if searching for something.

Dewey ducked out of sight, his mind racing as he struggled to put two and two together. Why were Clive and Amber in Milligan Creek—and together, no less? Dewey wasn't even aware they knew each other. He had no idea how Amber could be mixed up in all this, but he knew it couldn't be a coincidence. They had to be there searching for the case—and Dewey. But the previous night, Dewey had seen three people digging at the site, not two. If one of them was Clive and the other was Amber, then who was the third? Dewey froze in place as a single name flashed through his brain.

Earl.

17

A Startling Discovery

The orange early morning sunlight reflected off the front windows of the RCMP detachment as Staff Sergeant Romanowski pulled into his parking spot, momentarily blinding him. His eyes already bleary at the end of his long night shift, he squinted in the glare, only to see a flash of something in front of him. He slammed on his brakes, and when he looked up, standing before him and holding his umbrella out as if to protect himself from being hit by the cruiser was none other than Dewey Biggs.

Romanowski turned off his cruiser and got out. Before he could utter a word, Dewey dropped his umbrella and approached him, his fists pressed together and his palms up, as if begging to be handcuffed. "You've got to arrest me," he said. "Immediately."

"Why?" Romanowski asked, his hand going to his gun as he took a few steps back to create some space between him and Dewey while glancing around in case this was some kind of a setup. "What have you done?"

"Nothing! I mean . . . I don't remember. But I'm sure I did something bad."

Romanowski looked Dewey up and down and then

removed his hand from his weapon, unable to detect any sort of threat. "I'm sorry, but I can't arrest anyone without sufficient evidence. Not even you. Speaking of which, where have you been? I told you not to leave town, but I haven't been able to find you anywhere."

"What kind of evidence?" Dewey asked, casting a frightened look behind the staff sergeant as a car drove by, relaxing only slightly when he realized it wasn't the white New Yorker.

"Concrete, tangible evidence," Romanowski replied. "Something that can link you to the scene of a crime."

Dewey paused and thought for a moment. "Like this?" He picked up the umbrella and whacked the hood of Romanowski's cruiser.

"Now hold on a second," Romanowski said, stepping forward. "Damaging police property could earn you a hefty fine or six months in—"

Crash!

Romanowski's eyes widened in disbelief. Dewey had just used the handle of his umbrella to smash the cruiser's left headlight.

"That does it," he said, grabbing Dewey's arm. He spun him around and slammed him against the cruiser's hood, wrenching Dewey's arms behind his back and slapping his handcuffs on him. Despite his aggressive behavior seconds earlier, Dewey offered no resistance. In fact, if Romanowski could have seen Dewey's face, he would have seen a relieved smile cross his lips.

§

"Are you sure you're going to be OK, honey?" Mrs. Taylor asked as she stroked Matt's hair, which was slightly damp. "I hate leaving you at home when you're sick like this."

She held the back of her hand against his forehead to gauge his temperature. He was lying on the couch in their living room, a blanket pulled over him, all set up to spend the day watching TV. Mrs. Taylor had put a number of snacks, a glass of orange juice, and a pitcher of ice water within easy reach on the coffee table beside him. "You still feel a bit warm but not too bad. I'm just concerned about your heavy breathing. It's like you can't get enough air." With Chad keeping a lookout, Matt had just done several push-ups prior to her coming to check in on him. It had raised his body temperature slightly, though it also left him a bit breathless.

"You know what?" Matt said, swallowing hard to regain control of his breathing. "I think I'm starting to turn the corner."

"Don't worry, Mom," Chad said from the doorway to the living room. "I'll take good care of him."

"Oh yeah? I bet the minute we're out of here, you're going to be on the snowmobile off to get into mischief with your buddies," Joyce said as she breezed past on her way to the front door. Seeing as it was a long weekend due to Family Day, she and Mr. and Mrs. Taylor were about to head to Yorkton to do some shopping. The forecast for the next couple of days was good, so rather than drive, Mr. Taylor had decided to fly them there in his four-seat Cessna 172 airplane. Mrs. Taylor's parents lived in Yorkton and would loan them their car to get around once there, though they weren't too crazy about Mr. Taylor's driving—or Mr. Taylor, for that matter. They planned to stay overnight and return around noon the following day.

"That's what you think, Joyce!" Matt called out angrily

from the couch, not liking how close she was to the truth. When he saw Chad scowl at him, he suddenly remembered he was supposed to be sick and settled back onto the pillows and pretended to cough slightly.

"Oh, isn't that sweet, standing up for your big brother even when you're sick," Mrs. Taylor said, tousling Matt's hair.

"What a crock," Joyce retorted.

Just then, they heard the plane start up outside. "Well, I guess that's our signal," Mrs. Taylor said, standing up. "You boys be good. But I don't have to tell you that, do I? You're always good."

"That does it," Joyce said as she opened the front door. "I'm going outside."

"We will be, Mom," Chad assured his mother, giving her a hug. "Have a good trip."

Moments later, the boys watched out the living room's big picture window as Mr. Taylor taxied the plane out to the snow-covered grass runway that he had built in their field. Then he faced the plane into the wind, revved the engine, and sped down the runway. The minute the wheels left the ground, the boys leaped into action.

"That was easier than I thought it would be," Chad said as he and Matt threw on their snow gear.

"Except for Joyce sticking her nose into things," Matt said. "As usual."

Chad chuckled. "If she didn't do that, she wouldn't be Joyce."

"Well, we may have fooled them, but can we fool Dean?" Matt asked as he opened the closet and pulled out their matching snowmobile helmets.

Chad grinned as he took his from Matt. "There's only one way to find out."

§

While the Taylor boys were getting ready to continue working on the snow maze, Dean was at school putting a few final touches on his snow sculpture. It was pretty much his last opportunity to work on it prior to the sculptures being unveiled on Tuesday, and he wanted to make sure it was perfect. He had to fight his mother just to get that bit of time because she was eager to have him working on the snow maze, which also had to be completed by Valentine's Day.

As he stood back from it to get a bit of perspective, holding out his thumbs and forefingers like a film director framing up a shot, someone rapped on the blue tarp that served as a doorway to his cubicle. He whirled toward the sound, his eyes wild as he held out his arms to block the person's view of his sculpture. "Don't come in here!"

"I won't, dummy," Joy said. "It's against the rules to see anyone's sculpture before the big day, and I helped make up the rules. I just came by to see if you needed anything."

"No!" Dean replied. "I don't need anything!"

"Not even some hot chocolate?" she said, trying to make it sound as enticing as possible.

Dean opened his mouth to protest and then paused. He really did have a thing for hot chocolate. He pulled the blue tarp aside and stuck his head out, eyeing her suspiciously. "What about marshmallows?"

She held up a bag of fluffy white marshmallows and smiled as she dangled it in his face.

"Well, maybe one cup," Dean grumbled.

§

When Chad and Matt arrived at the snow maze site on their snowmobile, Andrew's snowmobile was already there, though there was no sign of him. Seconds later, he popped out of one of the tunnels, pushing a mound of snow in front of him. When he saw the boys, he stood up, took off his snowmobile helmet, and wiped his forehead. "Man, I never should have let Dean talk me into wearing this thing while digging. I'm cooking in here."

"Well, that was fast thinking to come up with that idea," Chad said.

"Maybe. Anyway, I'm glad you're here, Matt," Andrew said. "I think we're going to have to make some adjustments to your design."

"Why?" Matt asked as Andrew pulled out his hand-drawn map. "By the way, how long have you been here?"

"A while. Thought I'd get an early start seeing as there's so much to do. That's the problem. Even with your help, I still don't see how we'll possibly get it done in time. So I was wondering if maybe we could eliminate this section here," Andrew said, indicating a spot on the map. It featured a roundabout of sorts with several tunnels leading off in different directions, all of them except one leading to a dead end.

"Are you kidding me?" Matt replied. "That's one of my favorite parts."

"But we're going to have enough trouble digging all the tunnels that do lead somewhere, never mind the dead ends," Andrew replied. "Besides, it's bound to create a traffic jam if several people are going through that part at once, and they all have to turn back."

"It'll just add to the fun," Matt said, folding up the map

and handing it back to Andrew. "Now let's get digging. Time's a wasting."

Andrew sighed in defeat, knowing that arguing with Matt was pointless when he had a goal in mind.

§

Staff Sergeant Romanowski approached the RCMP station's holding cell with a cup of coffee and a blueberry muffin wrapped in cellophane. "You said two creams and one sugar, right?"

"Yes, thanks." Dewey took the coffee and muffin from Romanowski and then retreated to the bed, so he could sit down and eat.

Romanowski pulled up a chair and sat outside the cell, watching as Dewey tore the cellophane off the muffin. "So, care to tell me what that little episode was all about?"

Dewey looked up, having already bit into the muffin. He was ravenous. "Mphf thnot thure," he said through a mouthful of food. He paused to chew and swallow before continuing. "I'm not normally a violent person. Must have been something to do with my head injury. Some sort of fugue state or something."

"A fugue state," Romanowski said, unable to hide the skepticism in his voice as he nodded. "How about your memory? Getting any better?"

Dewey shook his head, his mouth full of muffin, then reached for his coffee to wash it down. When he was finished, he wiped his lips with the back of his hand. "But you never know, another one of these muffins might help."

Romanowski stared at Dewey in disbelief. Then he got up from his chair. If another muffin would make the little troublemaker talk, so be it.

§

"What would Dewey do? What would Dewey do? What would Dewey do?" Amber opened her eyes and looked at Clive as they drove down the highway. "See? I told you, for some reason it isn't working today."

"Oh yeah? And why do you suppose that is?" Clive asked. "Could it have anything to do with this?" He pulled a map of Saskatchewan out from under his coat. When Amber saw it, her eyes widened in surprise—and then fear.

"Where did you get that? I mean . . . what does that have to do with anything?"

"You tell me," he said, tossing it to her. "Show off your geography skills. See if you can find the town we were just in on the map for me."

"What's the point of that?" Amber asked, tossing the map back to him. "As if Dewey would hide out there."

"Just do it," he said in a tone that told her she had better obey.

"Fine. You don't have to get all huffy about it." She unfolded the map and searched it until she found Milligan Creek, Clive keeping his eye on her the entire time.

"Well? What about those arrows and that gibberish beside them? Read it for me."

The skin around Amber's eyes crinkled as she tried to sound out what was written in tiny block letters right beside Milligan Creek, along with two handwritten arrows. "Obinobitobials obon wobest sobide obof grobaveyobard gobate."

"What does it mean?" Clive asked.

Amber frowned, confusion overtaking the fear in her eyes. "It means we're going in the wrong direction."

Clive looked at her in shock. "What?"

18

A Weird Rock

With Matt and Chad's parents gone until the following day, the boys were prepared to dig all night if necessary to complete the snow maze in time. There was just one problem: Dean.

Though Chad and Andrew thought they should finally come clean with him about Matt's involvement, Matt disagreed. They were so close to the finish line now that he didn't want to risk anything coming between them and the completion of their snow maze. If they revealed that Matt had been part of the digging effort all along, not only would Dean be ticked off that they had deceived him, if he happened to mention that fact to his mother, she would probably show up with a bulldozer and level the place.

To maintain the illusion, seeing as Matt and Chad had matching snow gear and snowmobile helmets, all they had to do was make sure they were never seen in the same part of the snow maze at the same time. They also decided to divide and conquer, with each boy working on a different section, all of them digging toward a central hub that would eventually connect all the tunnels.

To keep in contact, Chad and Matt used walkie-talkies

with earpieces and keyed the mic when they planned to surface. One click meant "I'm coming out," two clicks in reply meant the coast was clear, and three clicks indicated whoever wanted to come out should stay under cover until the brother who was above the surface could disappear.

The system worked well for most of the day until Dean started to fall behind. Having already finished his tunnel, Andrew volunteered to go over and help him dig while Dean cleared out the snow using one of the escape hatches. Andrew had pre-cut and painted several pieces of plywood, which they had on site.

Pausing to take a breather, Dean flipped up the face shield of his helmet and gulped in the fresh air. He unzipped his snowsuit. He was cooking underneath it due to the work of digging. He was also concerned about how warm it was getting outside. With the temperature forecast to reach a degree or two above freezing over the next twenty-four hours, he worried about the condition of his snow sculpture. That last thing he wanted was for it to melt after all the hard work he had put into it.

Just as he was about to go back down and get another load, he saw an explosion of snow fly out of a tunnel several yards away, followed a moment later by "Chad," or so it appeared to Dean.

"How's it going?" Dean called out.

Looking a bit startled at first, Chad turned and responded with a thumbs-up.

"Almost finished?"

Chad held his hand flat and wobbled it back and forth to indicate he was neither here nor there. Then he disappeared back down into his hole.

"Thanks for the detailed update," Dean muttered sarcastically, about to pull his face shield back down. Suddenly, he saw "Chad" pop out of another hole several yards away from where he had just seen him. The instant he spotted Dean, he ducked back down.

"What the heck?" Dean exclaimed, unable to fathom how Chad could have possibly moved so quickly from one tunnel to the next. Then a realization struck him, causing his eyes to narrow. "Wait a second," he said, clambering out of his tunnel and throwing off his helmet.

§

Clive and Amber cruised slowly down Main Street in Milligan Creek, their eyes peeled for any sign of Dewey. However, all they saw were a couple of old men sitting on the bench outside the co-op grocery story, basking in the sunshine on the unseasonably warm day.

"Why on earth would Dewey hole up in this dump?" Amber asked, eyeing the ruins of the stores that had burnt that fall as a result of a grain elevator fire. "I mean, I know he's a loser, but still . . ."

Clive shrugged. "Beats me."

They had returned to Milligan Creek following Amber's decoding of the message on the map. As Clive suspected, her claim to have a psychic connection to Dewey had all been a ruse. Instead, she revealed that Dewey liked to play a game when he traveled. He'd stop at a service station in every town along the way. His first choice was Husky if the town had one—hence Amber's insistence on going there whenever possible. If the town didn't have a Husky, in descending order, he would go to Esso, Shell, Petro-Canada, Sunoco, Co-op, or Domo.

Once at the station, he would sneak a roadmap of Saskatchewan out of the rack. While pretending to look through it, he would draw an arrow beside the town where he was currently located, indicating which direction he was traveling. Then he would write a coded message that told where in town to find a hidden clue. The messages were written in something called the "ob language," which Dewey had learned as a kid. To use it, all a person had to do was put "ob" in front of the vowel sounds in every word. Thus, "Obinobitobials obon wobest sobide obof grobaveyobard gobate" meant "Initials on west side of graveyard gate."

For Dewey, it was like a scavenger hunt. He dreamed that one day a beautiful woman would stumble across his messages, decode them, and find her way to him. He believed that woman would be his soul mate, which was one of the reasons why Amber had broken up with him. Why bother dating if he didn't think she was his soul mate?

Once he came back through a town, Dewey would do the same thing, drawing an arrow in the opposite direction and leaving another clue. The fact there were two arrows on Milligan Creek but only one arrow on all the maps she had seen up to that point meant Dewey had gotten to Milligan Creek on his return trip and then stopped, though neither she nor Clive could fathom why.

"You think he has a friend or some family here?" Clive asked.

"How should I know?" Amber replied.

"You were his girlfriend for four months."

Amber sniffed. "Don't remind me."

When they reached the end of Main Street, Clive prepared to do a U-turn, ready to cruise the strip again in case they could spot Dewey walking around.

"Why don't you do your hospital/police station/post

office routine?" Amber asked. "And be quick about it. I'm getting hungry."

"I can't imagine how that could be possible," Clive said as he spotted a sign with a big letter H on it, indicating the hospital was to their right, and another sign with the profile of a police officer on it, indicating the RCMP detachment was to their left. Finally, he put on his signal light and turned.

§

Dewey was asleep in his cell when he was awoken by the sound of keys jangling. He sat up, bleary eyed, and saw an officer who he didn't recognize—Constable Chambers—unlocking the door.

"You're not Staff Sergeant Romanowski," Dewey said, though he did note Chambers also had an impressive mustache.

"No I am not," Chambers said. "But you're Dewey Biggs, and the big man says you're free to go."

Dewey's brow furrowed in confusion as Chambers held the door open for him. "What? But I damaged a police car. Intentionally."

"Yes, but technically that's just a mischief charge, which'll probably earn you a fine and probation when you appear in court." He handed Dewey a paper with his charges and court date on it. "And we don't keep people in jail for little things like that." He motioned for Dewey to come out of the cell.

Dewey's eyes darted around as his brain scrambled to come up with a reason to delay his release. There was no way he wanted to be walking around Milligan Creek with Clive at large, never mind Amber. He thought about tackling Constable Chambers and then immediately thought better of it. Not only would assaulting a police officer earn him serious jail time, Chambers was way bigger than him, and he already had a concussion. Best not to make it worse.

"My lawyer!" Dewey said, his mind finally hitting upon an idea. "I haven't talked to a lawyer yet. I'm not leaving here until I get my phone call. I know my rights." He got up and slammed the cell door shut with a clang.

The sound drew Rogers, who was also on duty, into the cell area. "There a problem here?"

"This guy doesn't want to leave," Chambers said. "Says he wants his phone call."

Rogers studied Dewey. He was a strange sight sitting on his bed with his hat and sunglasses on, his umbrella over his head. Normally, prisoners were stripped of all such items prior to being put into a cell, but Romanowski had made an exception for Dewey due to his concussion. "Well, normally people ask for that before they get released," Rogers said, "and they usually call their lawyer to avoid being put in jail, not because they want to stay, but I guess we can allow it."

§

Once he was out of his tunnel, Dean slithered across the snow, careful to avoid spots where they had excavated, so he wouldn't crash down through the roof of another tunnel. Once he reached Chad's tunnel, he dove inside and crawled until he reached the spot where Chad was digging.

"Aha!" Dean said. "I got you!"

Chad turned and looked at him. "What?" he said, his voice muffled slightly due to his helmet.

"Take off your helmet!"

"Why?"

"Just do it!"

Not knowing what else to do, Chad undid his chin strap and took his helmet off, careful to keep the side of his head with his walkie-talkie earpiece away from Dean. His hair was matted to his head due to sweat.

"Satisfied?" Chad asked, annoyed at the interruption.

"No!" Dean said. Then he turned and scrambled back down the tunnel.

Suddenly, Chad realized what was going on. He was about to follow Dean when he remembered the walkie-talkie. "Mayday! Mayday!" he said, keying the mic. "Matt, Dean's coming straight for you, and he's onto us!"

Dean burst out of the snow tunnel and headed straight for the area where Matt was digging.

"Yo, Dean, you have to check this out!" Andrew said, emerging from his tunnel.

"In a minute!" Dean said.

"No, I mean it. I found something strange!"

Dean paused. It wasn't like Andrew to get excited about anything. "Oh yeah, what is it?"

Andrew reached into the tunnel and pulled out a black hard-shell case. "This."

A moment later, Chad popped out of his tunnel, his helmet still off.

"What's in it?" Dean asked.

Andrew shrugged. "I haven't opened it yet. Come check it out."

His suspicions temporarily forgotten, Dean headed toward Andrew, followed by Chad.

§

Mrs. Muller was just putting on her snow boots when her husband, Dennis, came in from working in his shop, which was located in their oversized detached garage.

"Going somewhere, Audrey?"

"Yes," she replied, grunting as she struggled to pull on her left boot. "I'm going out to check on an investment."

"An investment? You made an investment without consulting me?"

"Oh, don't worry, Dennis. It didn't cost us any money. But it promises to create some huge returns—well, for me at least."

Dennis was about to inquire further but then decided against it. He knew better than to dig too deep when his wife was being cryptic like this. "But I thought we were going to eat lunch together."

"Lunch is on the stove," she said, standing up and heading toward the door. "I'm sure you can manage it on your own."

§

On their way to the police station, Clive and Amber passed Zee's Towing. Amber stared at the line of vehicles parked in his compound, all of them with their front end smashed in and a star-shaped crack on the driver's side of the windshield.

"What kind of vehicle did you say Dewey was driving again?" Amber asked.

"A blue station wagon," Clive replied, intent on reaching their destination. "A Dodge. A huge boat by the sound of it."

"Like that one?" she said, pointing to a blue Plymouth Fury station wagon at the end of the row of wrecks.

Clive looked to his right and then slammed on his brakes.

§

"Well, get on with it," Chambers said as Dewey stood by the phone, wondering who he should call. He didn't have a lawyer, a girlfriend, or any friends who had a phone, for that matter.

"Uh, do you have a phone book?" Dewey asked, stalling for time. He smiled weakly and tapped the side of his head. "The head injury. I'm having a hard time remembering anyone's number."

Chambers sighed. "Just a minute," he said, rooting around in his desk.

§

"What is it?" Dean asked as he slid into the tunnel with Andrew, Chad right behind him. "Hey, give me some room," Dean said as Chad's body blocked the entrance. "You're making me claustrophobic."

"Sorry," Chad said, moving to the side to allow a bit more daylight into the tunnel. "What'd you find, Andrew?"

In response, Andrew showed him the case. "I was digging my tunnel when my shovel hit something hard, and it sounded hollow. I thought it was some weird kind of rock, but when I dug around a little more, I found this."

"Well, open it!" Dean said, eager to see what was inside.

Andrew took off his mitts, fiddled with the latches,

and then opened the case.

"What's inside?" Dean asked, trying to see around the lid, which blocked his and Chad's view.

"I don't know," Andrew said as he spun the case around, so the other boys could see its contents. The case was lined with gray foam rubber, but it had two rectangular sections cut out at the center. Inside each cut-out was an object enclosed in a red velvet bag secured with a gold drawstring.

"Let me see one of those," Dean said, reaching for one of the bags.

"Wait!" Andrew said, grabbing Dean's arm as he paused to listen. "What's that?"

The other boys fell silent. Then they heard it too.

"A car," Chad said as the vehicle came to a stop and turned off its engine.

"So what?" Dean replied, shaking his arm free of Andrew. "I want to see what's in this bag."

"Hold on a minute," Chad said as he crawled to the tunnel entrance and peeked out. "It's not just any car," he said, turning and locking eyes with Andrew. "It's Dean's mother."

19

Site Inspection

The sound of Sarge barking drew Zee's attention away from his thirteen-inch black-and-white TV, where he had been watching the sports news in his office as he wolfed down a submarine sandwich. He looked out the window and saw a man and a young woman standing outside the gate to his lot.

"Now what the heck do they want?" he asked, reaching for his takeout cup and slurping down some Coke as he stood up to go out and greet them.

§

The bell over the door to Miriam's Flower Hut tinkled as the store's owner, Miriam Bondar, was finishing a huge floral arrangement for an upcoming funeral. When she looked up to see who it was, she was surprised to see Staff Sergeant Romanowski standing just inside the door and gazing around bashfully as if he were on completely unfamiliar turf—which he was.

"Richard!" the well-coiffed middle-aged woman said as she stepped out from behind the counter and wiped her perfectly manicured hands on her apron, which she wore to protect her designer dress. "What a pleasant surprise!"

"Hi, Miriam," he said, taking off his cap and nodding slightly as his face reddened.

She smiled at his nervousness. "What's the occasion?" she asked, trying to set him at ease. "I hope it's pleasure and not official police business."

Romanowski smiled weakly. "Actually, it's neither. And perhaps both."

She smiled and shook her head. "I don't think I quite understand."

"Well," Romanowski said, "what kind of flowers do I buy for a woman who is forcing me to go on a date with her that are nice enough to get me through the evening but don't give her or the other woman I'm dating the wrong impression?"

Miriam arched her left eyebrow and tilted her head to one side. Wanting to know more juicy details but patient enough to let them come out on their own, she turned and gestured for him to follow her. "Let's see what we can find in the cooler."

§

"Look, are you going to call someone or not?" Chambers said as Dewey continued to flip through the phone book. "I've got to get out on patrol, so get it done quickly or—"

"Couldn't you just put me back in the cell, even for a little bit?" Dewey asked. "I really could use the rest."

"That does it," Chambers said, standing up. "I'm taking you back to the hospital. Something is clearly wrong with your head, and we're not the people to deal with it."

§

"Well, well, well, you've been quite the busy beavers—or should I say gophers?" Mrs. Muller said as she stood and surveyed all the tunnel entrances that dotted the area.

"Most of those holes are going to be covered with plywood and snow," Chad explained, indicating the pile of white plywood sheets. "We're just using those entrances to excavate the snow right now. When it's finished, the maze will have three ways in but only one way out."

"And those hatches will work as emergency exits as well," Andrew reminded her. "Just in case someone gets really claustrophobic or a tunnel collapses, but we're confident neither of those things will happen."

"Don't worry, I have complete confidence in you boys," Mrs. Muller said. "Especially seeing as Matt's not involved." Chad and Andrew exchanged a concerned look, which did not go unnoticed by Dean. "Can you take me on a quick tour?" Mrs. Muller asked. "I just want to get a better sense of what the experience will be like."

"Yeah, great idea, Mom," Dean said. "Why don't we start right over there?" He pointed to the spot where Matt, disguised as Chad, had been digging. Chad was about to open his mouth in protest, but Mrs. Muller beat him to it.

"Way over there?" she asked. "Why can't we start right here?"

"Because, uh . . ." Andrew moved to block the entrance to the tunnel they had just come out of, not wanting her to go into it and see the hard-shell case, which they hadn't had time to hide. "Because it's, uh, it's not connected to the rest of the maze yet, so it won't give you the full effect. Here, let me show you another section . . ."

As Andrew led her away, Dean pulled Chad aside.

"Matt's here, isn't he?" he hissed. "He's been involved all along, hasn't he?"

Chad stared at him, not knowing how to respond. "Just help me hide the case before your mother gets back," he said finally.

Dean glared at the spot where he had seen Matt and then followed Chad into the tunnel.

§

"What can I do for you?" Zee asked as he approached the chain-link fence. Sarge had stopped barking at his master's appearance but was still growling at the newcomers. Amber reached her hand toward the fence to allow the dog to sniff it, but that only set off another round of barking and growling, forcing Zee to shush him.

"Good afternoon," Clive said once the barking subsided. "Sorry to disturb you, but that vehicle at the end." He pointed at the Fury. "How long has it been sitting there?"

Zee craned his head around to look at it and then turned back to Clive and Amber. "A few days. Owner went moose hunting with it. And you can see how that turned out." He grinned broadly at his well-worn joke as he looked Amber up and down and waggled his eyebrows at her. She scowled in disgust.

"And the owner?" Clive asked. "Is he OK?"

"Yes, he's—" Zee stopped. "Wait a second, how did you know the driver was a he?"

"Because he's my little brother," Clive replied. "And I've been looking everywhere for him. You don't happen to know where he is, do you?"

"Actually, I don't," Zee said. "But with the getup he's wearing, he shouldn't be too hard to find."

"Getup?" Clive said, glancing at Amber. "What sort of getup?"

§

"Honestly, I feel fine," Dewey insisted as Corporal Chambers drove him toward the hospital. "You don't have to do this."

"Well, you may feel fine, but you're acting pretty strange, and I'd rather have a doctor make a determination of your condition before I let you go out into the wild, if you know what I mean." Chambers glanced into his rearview mirror and then hit the brakes. Dewey, who had been in the back seat, was nowhere to be seen. "What the . . ."

"Is there a problem, officer?" Dewey asked.

Chambers turned around fully and realized Dewey was lying on the floor. He frowned. "What the heck are you doing down there?"

Dewey shrugged. "I, uh . . . I feel better down here. You know, the concussion and all."

"You just proved my point," Chambers said, turning around and hitting the gas. "I can't get you to the hospital soon enough."

After what—or rather who—he had just seen, Dewey couldn't agree more.

§

Outside Zee's towing, Amber and Clive had been mystified by the cruiser's sudden stop, thinking that perhaps the police were onto them somehow, only relaxing when it pulled away again.

"I can't believe I came face to face with the little twit

this morning and didn't even recognize him!" Amber said as they trudged back to the New Yorker.

"Yeah, well, at least we know he's here," Clive said, opening the car door for her in an uncharacteristic display of gentlemanliness. "And in this small town, it's only a matter of time before we run into him again."

§

Earl was livid. Not only were Dewey and the case still missing, Clive had stopped checking in, and even Meinhardt had gone AWOL after Earl had thrown the entire tea service at him in a fit of rage after being served one too many cups of pig swill that the gap-toothed grunt had dared to call tea. He didn't have anyone left in his organization who he trusted enough or deemed capable enough to go searching for Clive, never mind make tea for him, so he had no choice but to do the one thing he hated most. Rather than get someone else to do his dirty work, he would have to leave his office and do it himself.

He got up from his desk, opened the door and then . . . he closed it again. Despite his tough guy reputation, there was only one thing Earl hated more than doing things for himself, and that was leaving his office. Perhaps he'd wait on Clive a little longer.

Just then, his phone rang. He snatched the receiver off its cradle, eager for news—any news. "Hello?"

§

"You boys have done an incredible job," Mrs. Muller said as she clambered out of a tunnel and brushed the snow off her arms. "And in such a short time. I'm amazed how much you've accomplished seeing as only the three of you have been working on it." The comment earned another scowl from Dean, which he directed at Chad and Andrew, both of whom looked away. Mrs. Muller eyed the boys with suspicion as she observed their strange behavior. "There have only been three of you working on this, right? Matt is still at home sick in bed, right?"

"Seriously, Mom, do you really think Matt would pretend to be sick for days just so we could build a stupid snow maze?" Dean said. "Anyone who would do that would have to be out of his mind!" He practically shouted the last part in the hope that Matt would hear it from his hiding spot.

"OK, OK, you don't have to yell," Mrs. Muller said. "I believe you. Now, I want to let you boys get back to digging, but before I do, I have some thoughts on your admission price. Don't you think anyone who would be willing to pay three dollars would be willing to pay five dollars? I don't want to be greedy, but I want to make sure we don't leave any money on the table here . . ."

As she continued to talk, Dean rolled his eyes. As angry as he was at the other boys for deceiving him, he couldn't wait for her to leave, so they could finally find out what was inside that case.

§

"Your carriage has arrived," Constable Chambers said as he opened the rear door of the police cruiser to let Dewey out.

"You know, on second thought, I'd really prefer to keep riding around town with you, if that's all right," Dewey said, hunching down even further, so he couldn't be seen. “I’ve always wanted to see what a typical day in the life of a police office is like.”

“So you’re going to make this difficult, are you? All right then, come on . . .” Chambers reached into the back seat and grabbed Dewey’s arm. “Time to use some of those moves they taught me back in the academy.”

§

When Staff Sergeant Romanowski arrived home, he put the bouquet of flowers that he had bought for his date with Nurse Chaykowski in his fridge, just as Miriam had instructed him to do, and then quickly shut the door to remove the reminder of his guilt from his gaze. Then he opened the door and peeked at them again, the light from the fridge spilling over his stocking feet in the otherwise dark kitchen. For the umpteenth time, he told himself he should just call Henrietta and tell her what was going on, but not only did he feel terrible for letting things go as far as they had, telling her over the phone would only make her anxious and possibly decide to return home early, and there was no way he wanted to sabotage her opportunity to go on the mini-submarine expedition. No, he would just have to go through with the date, keep things as platonic as possible with Nurse Chaykowski, then tell Henrietta when she got home and let the chips fall where they may.

§

“How do you think they got there?” Matt asked as he and the others examined the contents of the hard-shell case.

All four boys were gathered around it on the plush red carpet in the Taylors’ living room. After Mrs. Muller finally left, Matt had come out of hiding, and he, Chad, and Andrew had confessed their duplicity to Dean. Though he was angry at being kept out of the loop, Dean agreed that his mother never would have let them go ahead with the snow maze if she knew Matt was involved. And now that it was almost complete, even Dean had to admit that what they had accomplished was impressive. Not only that, in between his work on the maze, he had been able to complete his snow sculpture as well, so he was riding high on thoughts of an upcoming romantic time at the dance with Joyce the following evening, which made forgiveness that much easier.

"The bigger question is, who put them there? And how long have they been there?" Chad said.

"And do they plan on coming back for them?" Dean added ominously, thinking about the strange-looking man with the umbrella that he thought he had seen the previous night.

The boys had decided that rather than open the case at the snow maze and be surprised by someone showing up again before they could hide it—or perhaps confronted by whoever had buried it in the snow—it would be safer to take it somewhere off site first.

"They can't have been there for long," Andrew said. "Look at the date."

Matt picked up one of the two rectangular grey objects up and examined it. They were printing plates, the kind use to make money. "You're right," he said. "It's dated this year." He slid his fingers over the engraving of Queen Elizabeth's face as well as the letters and numbers surrounding it and then set it back on the table with a satisfying thunk. "But why are they here in Milligan Creek?"

"We didn't find them in Milligan Creek," Dean reminded them, pulling both blocks of metal across the table toward him. “We found them on our land—my mother’s land, to be precise.”

“That doesn’t make them yours,” Matt said.

“Matt’s right,” Andrew confirmed. “They belong to the Canadian government. In fact, we could be in trouble for even having them in our possession.”

Dean slid the printing plates back across the coffee table, suddenly wanting them as far away from him as possible.

“Maybe we should just put them back,” Chad said.

Dean looked at him in alarm. “On my land? Are you kidding? No way.”

Matt scoffed. “Oh, so suddenly they’re not yours.”

“I don’t know guys,” Chad said. “I think we should take them straight to the police.”

“Or maybe,” Matt said, causing Chad to pause as he was about to scoop up the plates and put them back into the red velvet bags. “We should use them as bait . . .”

The other boys looked at him, curious to hear what he had in mind

20

The Big Reveal

"And finally, if you have any travel plans over the next few days, you may want to reconsider them in light of our three-day forecast. How 'bout it, Cindy? Tell us the good news first—if there is any." Channel Twelve news anchor Tucker Butker grinned as the camera cut to their meteorologist, Cindy Grossman, who smiled as she stood in front of a map of Saskatchewan.

"You want good news, Tucker? You got it. Today is Valentine's Day! Not only that, thermometers are about to climb above zero all across the province. Now for the bad news. Along with that warming trend will come some rain—yes, you heard me right, rain in the middle of February. What's the world coming to? In fact, it's already started in some regions of the province."

Dean looked up in alarm from where he had been shoveling Cheerios into his mouth at the kitchen table while half-listening to the broadcast. "Rain?" he said, spewing cereal across the table's green-and-white Formica surface. He reached over and yanked aside the lace curtain that covered the window. Sure enough, a light rain was already falling. His eyes flashed to the thermometer attached to the window frame outside. Even though it was overcast, the temperature had crept up to zero overnight. How could this be happening today of all days?

As Dean got up and took his dishes to the sink, then got ready to leave for school, Cindy continued her forecast. "But when the temperature drops again, which it will do this afternoon, expect that rain to turn to snow. In fact, many regions are in for a doozy of a blizzard that could last up to forty-eight hours, so maybe instead of going out to celebrate Valentine's Day this year, you should buy something special to cook at home, rent a romantic movie or two, and batten down the hatches. Oh, and don't forget chocolate!"

§

"How can that little creep stay out of sight for so long in a town as small as my pinkie toenail?" Amber asked as she applied bright pink nail polish to exactly that part of her foot. Clive had no idea why she bothered with such things when not only did she wear snow boots and/or wool socks 100 percent of the time due to her feet always being cold, they were in a hurry to track down Dewey before he left town—if he hadn't left already after his surprise encounter with Amber at the service station. As Clive examined Amber further, he realized that not only had she painted her toenails, she had also painted her fingernails, done her hair nicely, and put on makeup.

"It looks like you're getting ready to go on a date," Clive observed.

Amber glared at him. "Maybe I am. Not that it's any of your business. Besides, a girl doesn't need to be going on a date to want to look her best, you know. In fact, you should try it sometime." She looked him up and down and curled her lip in disgust at his rumpled clothes. "Looking your best, that is. I can't imagine why anyone would want to go on a date with you."

Clive huffed in exasperation. "Can we just get going?"

"Where?" Amber asked, waving her hand at her foot to dry the nail polish. "We've already been all over this dump, and you've put Dewey's picture up all over town. Why don't we just get some breakfast and then come back here and watch TV as we wait for someone to turn him in?"

"Because I just realized there's one place that we haven't checked yet that should have been obvious," Clive said.

"Oh yeah? Where's that?"

"You'll have to come with me to find out," Clive replied. "And from what I've heard, they have a machine there that sells Jimmy Deans . . ."

§

Dean raced up to the snow sculpture enclosure, breathless from running halfway across town, and then stopped when he saw a beehive of activity. Mr. Karky and several other volunteers were struggling to stretch extra tarps over the structure to protect the sculptures from the rain.

"Don't just stand there, Muller, lend a hand!" Mr. Karky said as he secured the corner of one tarp to a nail that had been pounded into the structure.

"Moo!" Ben added as he tried to do the same with another corner. Dean rushed in to help the struggling boy.

"My sculpture, is it—"

"It's fine!" Joy said in a sing-song voice as she emerged from the structure.

"Wait a second," Dean said, releasing the corner of the tarp and allowing it to flap in the wind, Ben leaping up and down as he tried to grab it again. "You didn't look at it, did you?"

"Of course not," Joy said, smiling sweetly. "That would be a violation of the rules."

"Good," Dean said, grabbing the tarp again, ending Ben's frantic chorus of "moos."

§

Dennis Muller's eyes were still a bit bleary from sleep as he tramped out to his workshop to prepare for his day, thankful for the unseasonably warm weather seeing as he was going to be working outside.

As he approached his workshop, he realized a light was on inside. Thinking he had forgotten to turn it off the night before, when he opened the door, he was surprised to find his wife inside cleaning out a paintbrush in the industrial sink.

"Good morning, Dennis," she said, her face bright with excitement.

"What are you doing in here?" Dennis asked, looking around for a hint of what she had been up to. "I thought you had gone out for a walk." He paused and sniffed, the air full of paint fumes. "You know, you really should open the overhead door if you're going to paint," he said, walking over and pressing the button that activated it.

"No time," Mrs. Muller replied, scooping up a large, flat bundle wrapped in a tarp. She also grabbed a bundle of sticks, a hammer, and a package of nails.

"Dare I ask what you're up to?" he inquired as she ducked under the ascending garage door, too impatient to wait for it to rise all the way.

She paused and looked back. "That all depends," she

replied cryptically. "How badly do you want to know?

Dennis considered it momentarily and then waved. "Have a good morning, Audrey."

"You too, Dennis," she said, smiling sweetly as he hit the button to bring the garage door back down.

§

Normally, Staff Sergeant Romanowski looked forward to his days off, but today he would have given anything to have a big case to solve, something so extraordinary that it put Milligan Creek on the map and his face on every major news broadcast across the province, if not the country. Anything would have been better than having to spend the entire day dreading his date with Nurse Chaykowski that evening.

Unable to come up with anything better to do, he settled onto his couch with a second cup of coffee and turned on the TV, catching the tail end of a weather forecast. A blizzard was coming. Great. Maybe the dinner would be called off. Aw, who was he kidding? He, Nurse Chaykowski, and Dr. Maharaj all lived in town, so it would be no problem to walk. Somehow, he knew this date was going to happen no matter what.

§

"The hospital? This is your big idea?" Amber said as she and Clive pulled into a parking spot. "We already know he's not in the hospital. I saw him at the gas station yesterday, remember?"

"Yes, but he's got a concussion—a bad one by the sound of it. Maybe he checked himself back in."

Clive went to open his door, but Amber grabbed his arm. "Wait a second. What are you going to do?"

"Isn't it obvious?" Clive replied. "I'm going to look for Dewey."

"No, after you find him," Amber said.

Clive stared at her. He'd been so caught up in finding Dewey that he hadn't quite thought that part through. In that instant, he realized that whatever he had planned for Dewey, now Amber was wrapped up in it too.

"He took something that didn't belong to him," Clive said, "and I'm going to take it back."

"And then?"

Clive looked out the window as an Indo-Canadian man dressed in medical scrubs hurried out to his car. "We'll cross that bridge when we come to it," he said finally.

§

"I still think we should have just taken them straight to the police," Chad said as he, Matt, and Andrew entered the school.

"I agree," Andrew replied.

"There's nothing to worry about," Matt assured them. "Except this stupid rain. I just hope it doesn't ruin the snow maze."

"It shouldn't," Andrew said. "The tunnels may shrink a bit if this warm weather keeps up, but it's forecast to start cooling again by noon, which should turn this rain back to snow."

"And bring a blizzard along with it, so no one will be able to go through the maze tonight," Chad pointed out.

"We could always postpone it," Andrew suggested. "In fact, maybe we should."

"No way," Matt said. "Things could be even worse

by then."

"Um, are you guys forgetting something?" Chad asked. "The case?"

"You worry way too much," Matt said. "We wiped everything down, so none of our fingerprints are on the case or the printing plates, and we put it right back where we found it. Now all we have to do is place a lost-and-found ad, and then—" His words were cut off as the bell rang.

"I still think it's a stupid idea," Chad said as they parted ways toward their classrooms. "Let's talk about it again at noon."

Matt groaned in frustration. "You guys have no sense of adventure!"

§

Clive did a double take when he entered the hospital and nearly ran into an Indo-Canadian doctor dressed in medical scrubs, who was on his way out. Clive stopped short and looked back toward the parking lot. "Wait a second, didn't I just see you . . ."

"Can I help you?" Dr. Maharaj asked, holding the door open for Clive and Amber. Clive finally shook his head, thinking he must have been seeing things.

"Oh, uh, we're looking for . . . my little brother. I hear he may be a patient here."

"The nurse at the front desk should be able to help you," Dr. Maharaj said. "I'm sorry, I'd look into it for you, but I'm on my way out to do my rounds at the nursing home."

"No problem," Clive said, stepping aside, so the doctor could pass. "We can find our way."

"You mean you can find your way," Amber said, pushing past him. "I'm getting breakfast."

§

Dean was giddy as he stood by his desk waiting for "O Canada" to end. As soon as it did, it would be time for morning announcements, the biggest of which would be about the unveiling of the snow sculptures, which would happen almost immediately at a special outdoor assembly that morning. It was supposed to happen at noon, but considering the warming weather, the event had been moved up. Dean was confident the tarps would keep his sculpture dry, but the thermometer was continuing to climb, which had him worried it could still melt before he had a chance to unveil it to the world—and most importantly, to Joyce. However, with circumstances beyond his control, all he could do was wait.

§

"I'm sorry, sir, but we don't divulge information like that about any of our patients," Nurse Chaykowski said from her post at the hospital's front desk.

"But he's my little brother," Clive pleaded, using his most sympathetic tone. "He's been missing for days. The entire family is worried sick about him."

"Your little brother, you say . . ." Nurse Chaykowski's eyes narrowed. "Was he raised in Britain too? Does he have an accent like you?"

Clive silently kicked himself for not thinking through that part of his plan.

As he launched into a convoluted explanation about how he and Dewey had been raised on separate continents by different parents, Amber made her way over to the food machines in the main waiting room.

"That stupid jerk!" she exclaimed.

Contrary to Clive's claims, none of them contained Jimmy Dean meals. In fact, all they had to offer was chips, candy bars, and sodas. It wasn't like Amber was averse to such fare, but even she had her limits, especially after Clive had gotten her hopes up for something else.

She was just about to head back to the front desk and chew him out when she was distracted by a sound that she rarely encountered inside of a hospital: giggling.

She looked up and saw some candy stripers gathered outside a patient's room, smiling and waving at whoever was inside. Curious, she glanced at Clive, who was still engaged with the nurse at the front desk, and then wandered toward the room. When the candy stripers saw her approaching, they hustled away to resume their duties.

Amber peeked through the window in the door. It was quite dark inside, but she could just make out the silhouette of a figure on the bed. Three details stood out immediately: a hat, a pair of sunglasses, and an umbrella. With a final look back toward Clive, she opened the door and slipped inside.

§

"All right, ladies and gentlemen, settle down, or we'll just send you back inside and cancel the whole thing!" Mr. Karky shouted as the entire student body assembled around the ramshackle structure that concealed the snow sculptures. The students quieted somewhat in response. Some of them were eager to see the big reveal, some of them were bored, some were annoyed at being made to stand outside in the light rain, and others were simply happy to have a few minutes off class.

“Each student can cast three votes using the tickets you received in your home room,” Mr. Karky said. “You can spread them out between your three favorite sculptures or put all three on one. And remember, all the sculptors put a lot of work into these creations, so show some respect. OK, sculptors, are you ready?”

“Yes!” they replied in unison, each one posted outside the structure at the spot where their sculpture was located.

“OK, three, two, one!” Mr. Karky pulled a rope, and due to a clever mechanism that Mr. Peesker, the shop teacher, had rigged up, the tarps fell away, revealing the snow sculptures, each sculptor standing proudly in front of his or her creation. Of all the sculptors present, Dean’s smile was the biggest of all.

§

Dewey was so tired from the medication the doctor had given him, and his sunglasses were so dark that when he saw a female figure enter his room, at first, he thought he was dreaming—or hallucinating. But as the figure drew closer to his bed, he realized it was probably a nurse or one of those pesky candy stripers.

He went to take off his sunglasses. “I’m sorry, but I don’t need any—”

“You stupid, boneheaded dork.”

The moment he heard that voice, he dropped his hand. He didn’t need to remove his sunglasses to know who it was.

“Amber? What are you doing here? How did you—” He looked past her as a bolt of fear shot through him. “Clive. Where is he?”

She glanced back toward the door. “Never mind him.

You need to get out of here. Now."

"What? Why? Where—"

"And when you get out of here, go straight to Saskatoon and return whatever you took from Earl. Even then I think it might be too late."

"But I didn't take anything! Wait a second, I saw you with Clive," Dewey said. "Why were you—"

"Don't worry about that. Just get moving."

"OK, OK," Dewey said, pulling back his covers as he tried to clear his head.

§

Dean beamed as he stood with his back to his sculpture, his entire body humming with excitement as he waited for Joyce to come by and cast her vote.

He looked down the line at some of the other sculptures. Ben and Zoey's consisted of two black-and-white Jersey cows being milked in a stall by two people who looked remarkably like Ben and Zoey. How they had created black snow was a mystery to him.

Next to them, a large crowd of students who were freaking out partially obscured the next sculpture.

"Eww!" A girl screamed. "Disgusting!"

As she stepped aside, Dean caught sight of what looked to be a snowman. It had a corn-cob pipe, a button nose, and two eyes made out of coal. There was just one problem. Unlike the frosty, glistening snow that made up all the other sculptures, this snowman wasn't white at all. Instead, he was a blazing, alarming, disturbing shade of yellow.

"It's not what you think it is!" the sculpture, Randall Soll, shouted. "Taste it! Taste it!"

He scooped a handful of snow out of the snowman's

belly, but no one would take him up on it, even after he put some in his mouth.

"I should give you detention for a month for creating a monstrosity like that," Mr. Karky said. "That does it. Next year all snow sculptures will require staff approval."

"But Mr. Karky," Randall pleaded. "It's not made of—"

"I don't care what it's made of," Mr. Karky said. "You're disqualified."

Dean returned his attention to the crowd gathered around his sculpture. Some of the students were pointing at it and giggling. He didn't mind though. He had expected that sort of response. He didn't care what they thought. All he was worried about was one person . . .

"My answer is yes, Dean!" a female voice cried. "I will!"

Dean smiled. This was working out just as he had imagined it. His eyes searched the teeming mass of students for the source of the voice. As they did, his brain finally caught up to his eyes, only then realizing that the voice didn't belong to Joyce, as he thought when he first heard it. There was no mistaking it now. That voice belonged to . . .

"Joy?" Dean said as his eyes finally settled upon her beaming face.

"Yes! A thousand times yes!" Joy gushed as she emerged from the crowd. "If I had known this was what you were up to all along . . ."

Dean shook his head in confusion. "But I didn't make it for you. I made it for—"

He turned to look at the sculpture. It featured Snoopy and Woodstock from the Peanuts cartoon strip dancing together. Beneath it in big block letters were the words "Will you be my Woodstock tonight, Joy?" Dean's mouth fell open in alarm. "It's supposed to say Joyce! Joyce, not Joy! What happened . . ." That's when he realized the C and the E in "Joyce" had fallen over, likely due to the warming temperature.

He rushed over to see if he could fix it. "Wait, there's been a mistake!" he said as he quickly tried to stand them back up, but the letters just fell apart in his hands. He stood up. "Mr. Karky! I want to withdraw my sculpture from the contest!"

Mr. Karky shook his head resolutely. "Too late!"

"Nice job on Woodstock, Dean," Joyce said as she emerged from the crowd and slipped a ticket into the box beside his sculpture. "I sure wish I had someone as romantic as you to take me to the dance tonight." She smiled and winked at him before moving on.

"But Joyce, you do! There's just been a mistake . . ." Dean said weakly, falling to his knees as she disappeared into the crowd.

"The only mistake I see is me thinking you'd never ask," Joy said as she stepped up beside him and fluttered her eyelashes. "Not to mention you waiting for so long to do it. But doing it like this makes up for everything." She held out her hand to help him to his feet. He looked at it for a moment, then sighed and took hold of it.

21

Build-up to the Big Night

Clive was livid. Not only had the nurse refused his repeated requests for information about Dewey, now he had lost track of Amber. He was doing a final sweep through the waiting room when he saw a patient door open down the hall and someone peek out. On a whim, he slipped behind a vending machine and watched as a female figure checked to see if the coast was clear and then gestured for someone to follow. A male figure emerged from the room, and they headed down toward the far end of the hall, straight toward an emergency exit.

Clive stepped out from behind the vending machine to follow them and then stopped as an idea struck him, deciding to go out the front door of the hospital instead.

§

"You really faked us out with Joy," Matt said as he and the other boys headed back to class following the sculpture reveal. He put his arm around Dean's shoulders. "If I didn't know better, I would have thought you hated her. And just think, all along I thought you were going to use the snow sculpture to ask out my sister."

"For the last time," Dean said, shrugging off Matt's arm. "The sculpture was supposed to say 'Joyce.'"

"Sure it was," Matt said, grinning. He ducked as Dean swung at his shoulder and missed.

"So, if you're taking Joy to the dance tonight, does that mean you won't be coming out to the snow maze?" Chad asked.

"Of course I'm coming," Dean said. "I'm the only one my mom trusts to collect the ticket money."

They had announced the snow maze following the sculpture contest and had gotten a great response from the students, who were all excited to give it a try after the dance that night.

"Let's just hope the weather holds up," Andrew said, glancing out the window.

§

Dewey kept glancing in the side-view mirror as he and Amber rode down the highway with Zee in his tow truck, Dewey fearing that any minute now, he would see the white New Yorker roaring up behind them.

"Quit acting so strange," Amber whispered as they passed a crudely painted wooden sign that said, "Snow Maze – Only 1 More Mile!"

They had asked Zee to drive them back to the scene of the accident, ostensibly so Dewey could show the spot to Amber, his "grieving girlfriend," who had supposedly assumed Dewey was dead. They didn't bother mentioning that she had merely wished Dewey had gone to the great beyond.

Zee slowed his truck as they reached the spot. "Here

you be," he said. "Moose smear and all." He indicated the bloody spot on the road, which was already fading due to all the traffic driving over it.

"Do you mind if we . . . if we spend a bit of time here?" Dewey asked.

Zee looked at his watch. "Well, I got some things to do back in town, but I suppose I could spare a few minutes."

"No, not you. You've already been so kind," Amber said, fluttering her eyelashes at him. "And we wouldn't dream of taking up any more of your time. We'd just like to spend a few minutes at the spot where my Dewey-whewy almost died. Then we'll walk back to town. It'll be romantic."

Zee thought about it and then shrugged. "Suit yourself," he said. "At least it's warm out."

"Thanks, Zee," Dewey replied as he opened the door.

"Yes, thank you so much," Amber said, putting her hand on Zee's arm, which caused him to blush a fiery red.

"Don't mention it," he replied, barely able to choke out the words.

§

Mrs. Muller grunted as she pounded the final sign for the snow maze into the snow on the side of the road. She had spent the morning installing several of them between Milligan Creek and the maze, so customers would have no problem finding their way.

As she stood back to admire her handiwork, she saw two figures approaching down the road—a woman and a man who was carrying . . .

"An umbrella? In February? Hmph. Takes all kinds."

She waited until they were within earshot before addressing them. "Sorry, but if you're here for the snow maze, we don't open until tonight."

The couple stopped, as if surprised to see her. They conferred quietly with each other before the woman turned back to Mrs. Muller.

"Um, we're here from the, uh, the Yorkton newspaper. We heard about the snow maze, and we want to do a story on it."

"You're from the Enterprise?" Mrs. Muller replied, eyeing them skeptically. "Where's your camera? And where's your car?" She looked past them down the empty road.

The couple looked at each other. The man shrugged. The woman scowled at him before turning back to Mrs. Muller. "Uh, our cameraman is on his way. He dropped us off at the highway. We thought it was a nice day for a walk. We just wanted to preview the maze before anyone else went through it."

"Sorry, no can do," Mrs. Muller said. "This maze is on my property, and if you want to go through it, you'll have to wait like everyone else—and pay the five-dollar entry fee. Can't risk anyone wrecking it before our customers show up. As the landowner though, I'd be happy to grant you an interview."

Dewey and Amber looked at each other as Mrs. Muller approached. This was definitely more than they had bargained for.

§

"A door is ajar. A door is ajar . . ."

Clive slammed the New Yorker's trunk and then walked around and kicked its front-left tire, which hurt his foot, seeing as the tire was completely flat. Of all the times for him to forget to pump it up in the morning. His plan had been to sneak out to the car and follow Amber and Dewey, hoping they would lead him to the case, but now they were long gone, and he was stuck in the hospital parking lot. Now what was he going to do?

"A door is ajar. A door is—"

"Shut up!" he yelled, kicking the driver's door shut, only to realize he had just locked his keys in the car. Furious, he stood there and considered his options, then trudged back into the hospital in search of a payphone.

As he walked, the light raindrops that had been falling transformed into tiny flakes of snow.

§

That evening, Staff Sergeant Romanowski took a deep breath as he stood in front of the mirror in his bathroom. He was dressed in his best suit—a brown tweed number with a blue shirt and a bright orange tie. He had bought it several years earlier when he was the best man at a friend's wedding. It still fit, but it was snugger in some places than he would have liked. Time to begin hitting the treadmill down at the station.

He leaned forward and wiggled his upper lip, making sure all the hairs in his mustache were impeccably trimmed, which they were. In truth, he knew he was merely trying to forestall the inevitable. He looked at his watch and sighed. It was 5:30. Time to get this over with . . .

§

"Seriously, Mom, I think I'm coming down with something," Dean said.

"Oh no you're not," Mrs. Muller replied as she adjusted Dean's clip-on bowtie and then stood back to examine his overall appearance. "You're taking that nice girl to the dance, and then you're collecting ticket money at the snow maze, and Matt Taylor won't ever see a penny of it, even though the entire thing was his idea." She chuckled at the thought of it.

"But Mom, I could die of pneumonia."

She paused and glared at him, midway through brushing some lint off his shoulder. "You wouldn't dare."

Dean looked into her eyes and swallowed hard. "No, ma'am, I wouldn't."

§

"I can't believe that worked," Amber said as she and Dewey killed time walking down a side street back in Milligan Creek. "That woman was so gullible. Crazy but gullible." A light snow was falling, causing Amber to squint as the breeze blew the flakes into her eyes. "Here, give me that." She grabbed Dewey's umbrella, which she figured he no longer needed now that the sun had dipped below the horizon, and used it to deflect the snow.

"We know who the kids are and where to find them, but we still don't know if they have the case," Dewey pointed out, shielding his eyes against the sun's receding orange glow.

"Of course they have the case," Amber replied. "You said so yourself. One of those snow tunnels comes out right under the padlock."

"Yeah, but that woman didn't seem to know anything about it."

Amber stopped and glared at Dewey. "Think about it, dipstick. If you were a kid, and you found that case, would you tell your parents about it?"

Dewey thought about it and then shrugged. "No, I guess not." Then he looked around uneasily. "I still don't understand what happened to Clive though."

Amber scoffed. "That nitwit? He couldn't find a snowflake in a snowstorm."

§

"Don't you look sharp," Nurse Chaykowski said as she opened the door to find Staff Sergeant Romanowski on her front step. He was wearing his RCMP-issue parka over his suit along with his muskrat-fur hat, the earflaps tied up on top. She glanced at her watch. "And right on time too."

He held out some flowers. "Here. These are for you."

"Oh, you're so sweet," she said, her white teeth flashing in contrast to her bright red lipstick, which matched her dress. "Why don't we bring them with us? Then we can enjoy them during dinner."

"Suit yourself," Romanowski said, holding out his elbow. She slipped her arm through his.

"Ooh, such a gentleman."

"Now that I'm here, care to tell me which doctor's house we're going to?"

She grinned up at him. "Wouldn't you like to know."

He sighed and then led her out to his police cruiser, both of them ducking their heads against the intensifying snowfall.

22

The Big Date

Music was pumping through the walls of the Milligan Creek Composite School gymnasium as a stream of excited, chattering students filed inside for the Cupid Is As Cupid Does dance. Among them were Andrew, Chad, and Matt. Typically, none of the three boys would have attended such an event, but they wanted to be there to remind students to come out to the snow maze afterwards and to make sure they actually did.

"Where's Dean?" Matt asked, looking around.

"Right over there," Chad said, pointing. The other boys watched as Dean's mom got out of her van, which was parked at the end of the sidewalk in full view of all the students. She walked around and opened the sliding door for Dean and Joy, then popped open an umbrella and held it up to protect them from the falling snow.

"Wow," Matt said. "Talk about red carpet service."

"Something's red all right," Chad replied with a grin. "And it's not the carpet!"

The other boys laughed as Dean got out of the van, his cheeks a blazing crimson due to all the attention he was getting.

"Mom, this is embarrassing. You can go now," Dean said through clenched teeth as he attempted to smile at the many students who were gawking at him as he helped Joy out of the van.

"It's not embarrassing at all," Joy said as she emerged from the vehicle, dressed in a bright pink satin princess dress with puffy sleeves, a tiara studded with fake diamonds glistening in her hair. "It's wonderful. What an entrance!"

"Stop right there," Mrs. Muller said. Before Dean could reply, she snapped a photo of him and Joy with a Polaroid camera. "Aw, you make such a cute couple," she said, snapping another one.

"Mom, we're not a couple!" Dean hissed. "I wasn't even supposed to—"

"Have a great time!" Mrs. Muller said, already heading around to the driver's side of the van. "And remember, I'll be back here to pick you up as soon as the dance is over to take you out to the snow maze." Huge, wet snowflakes pelted her face as she looked up at the sky, a light wind causing them to swirl. "I just hope this snowfall doesn't get any worse."

"Thanks for the ride, Mrs. Muller!" Joy said. She turned to Dean, her face beaming. "Shall we?" she asked, holding out her hand.

"I am not holding your hand," Dean said.

Just then, Mrs. Muller rolled down the passenger window behind them. "One more thing, Dean," she said. "Be a gentleman." She scowled and nodded for him to take Joy's hand.

Dean tilted his head back and groaned in frustration. "For Pete's sake!" He grabbed Joy's hand and yanked her toward the front entrance. Joy's smile couldn't have been wider, enjoying his bashfulness as well as the fact that all the other students were looking at them.

As Dean walked, trying not to meet anyone's gaze, he looked off into the distance—and then stopped short, nearly causing Joy to run into him.

"Dean, what are you doing?" Joy whispered through clenched teeth, forcing a smile as she tugged on his hand. "Everybody's watching."

"What? Oh, nothing," he said, staring at the spot again before yanking Joy forward, causing her to stumble as she hurried to keep up with him. "I need to find my friends. Now!"

"Do you think he saw us?" Dewey asked as he and Amber ducked behind the corner of the school.

"How could he not with your stupid umbrella?" she said. "Put that thing away."

"But it helps protect my eyes," Dewey replied, pointing at the spotlight illuminating the tennis court behind them.

"I don't care about your eyes. You can protect them later. We know what the kid looks like. Now all we need to do is get into that dance."

"How are we going to do that?" Dewey asked.

Amber peeked around the corner again and then smoothed her hair. "Leave that to me."

§

Romanowski parked his cruiser outside of a modest split-level home, having followed Nurse Chaykowski's directions there. He turned off the ignition and smacked the steering wheel in triumph. "So it was Harpreet who invited me. I knew it!"

“Did you?” she asked, a skeptical smile on her face.

He opened his mouth to answer and then thought better of it. “Let me get the door for you.”

She chuckled to herself as he got out and walked around the front of the vehicle, then opened her door. “My, my, you really are pulling out all the stops, aren’t you?”

He blushed as he took her hand and helped her out of the vehicle, a light snow dusting the top of his fur hat.

Moments later, they were standing on Dr. Maharaj’s front steps, waiting for someone to answer the doorbell.

“Mmm . . . I can smell that curry already, can’t you?” Nurse Chaykowski asked as she rubbed her hands together, a teasing smile on her lips. “What a great way to cap off Valentine’s Day.”

Romanowski grunted as he saw someone approaching the door inside, the person’s outline blurred by the sidelight’s mottled glass. “Just a word of warning, I never like to stay too late at these . . . things.”

His pause was precipitated by the fact that when the door opened, it revealed not Dr. Maharaj or his wife, Gurvinder, but Henrietta!

Romanowski stared at her, slack-jawed. Not only was he completely flummoxed to encounter Henrietta at Dr. Maharaj’s house, for perhaps the first time ever, she was wearing a dress—and makeup. And in Romanowski’s eyes at least, she looked spectacular.

“But Henrietta. . . what are you . . . why are you . . .” He suddenly remembered Nurse Chaykowski standing beside him, clearly all dolled up for a date. “Oh, wait, this isn’t what it looks like. I mean I never—”

“Thanks, Sharon,” Henrietta interrupted. “I can take things from here.” She smiled as Nurse Chaykowski handed her the flowers that Romanowski had given her. “Oh, how nice!" Henrietta exclaimed. The stunned staff sergeant stared at the two women in disbelief as they shared a brief hug. "Thanks for everything!" Henrietta said.

"No problem," Nurse Chaykowski replied as she descended the steps, waving to the couple. "Happy Valentine's Day!"

"Do you want me to give you a lift home?" Dr. Maharaj asked, sticking his head out the door. He grinned at Romanowski. "Good evening, Richard. Surprised?"

"To put it mildly," Romanowski replied, his mustache bristling.

"No, I'm fine to walk," Nurse Chaykowski said. "It's a beautiful night!"

"It certainly is," Henrietta said, taking Romanowski's hand. "Now let's get inside out of this snow. You won't believe what Harpreet and Gurvinder have cooked up for us!" She gave him a peck on the lips.

With a final glance at Nurse Chaykowski, Romanowski smiled at Henrietta. "So you set this entire thing up?"

She shrugged. "With a little help from my friends."

He grinned and shook his head. "Happy Valentine's Day, Henrietta."

"Same to you, Richard."

They shared a longer kiss on the front porch before heading inside out of the snow, which was already falling even harder than when Romanowski arrived.

§

"I'm serious, guys, the crazy person with the umbrella, I just saw him outside!" Dean shouted over the pounding rock beat. The other boys weren't sure what to make of his claim. Their faces illuminated by flashing disco lights, they were clustered along the wall with dozens of other boys, most of the girls having taken up a position on the opposite side of the gymnasium. Despite the blaring music, so far only a few couples had been brave enough to hit the dance floor.

"But why would he be hanging around outside a school dance?" Matt asked.

Dean stared at Matt as if he needed to have his head examined. "Why do you think? Because he knows we have the case!"

"Do you think we should call the police?" Chad turned to Andrew, whose eyebrows were knit together in concentration.

"And tell them what?" Matt inquired before Andrew could formulate a reply. "Walking around with an umbrella isn't a crime, even if it is February."

"Tell them about the case," Dean said. "Like we should have in the first place."

"There you are!" a female voice said. All four boys turned to see Joy's smiling face, the disco lights causing her tiara to glisten with a myriad of colors. "You're not trying to ditch me, are you?" She reached for Dean's hand, but he pulled it away.

"What are you doing?" he asked.

"I want to dance," she replied as "You Give Love a Bad Name" by Bon Jovi ended and the open chords of Abba's "Waterloo" began. "This is one of my favorite songs. In fact, I just requested it."

"Not now," Dean said. "I'm busy."

Joy crossed her arms and frowned. "Your mom told you to be a gentleman, did she not?"

"Yes, but—"

"You wouldn't want me to have to tell her you weren't

a gentleman, would you?" Before Dean could respond, she grabbed his hand and yanked him toward the dance floor, a number of other couples doing the same as the song heated up. "Now stop being so silly, and come dance with me!"

"Don't worry, Dean!" Matt called out after him as Dean looked back helplessly. "We'll think of something!"

23

Kidnapped

"I'm sorry, Ms. Applebottom, but I don't see your name on the list of chaperones. How'd you say you were related to Dean again?" Mr. Peesker, who was manning the front door, ran his finger down the list of chaperones one more time.

Amber smiled her brightest smile, doing her best to put on a fake Australian accent, though her voice kept waffling between sounding like she was from Down Under and like she was from somewhere deep in the American South. For some reason, Mr. Peesker didn't seem to notice. "Why, I'm his Aunt Beulah from Adelaide, and I'm here to visit my little nephew and his family. This is my first time in Canada. In fact, it's the first time I've ever seen snow. Isn't it wonderful?"

Mr. Peesker looked out the wall of glass doors, where the snow was really coming down. "Yes, quite." He sat back and gave Amber a once-over. "Well, I could call Mrs. Muller to confirm, but we wouldn't want to get on Audrey's bad side now, would we?"

Amber stared at him blankly, then suddenly twigged on to the fact that Audrey was the name of Dean's mother. "Definitely not!" she exclaimed, her voice and her mannerisms overly dramatic. "Why, when my sister goes on a tear, watch out!"

Mr. Peesker smiled as he stepped aside to let her pass. "Indeed. Thank you for volunteering to help out. And enjoy your stay in Canada!"

"Thank you!" Amber said as she hurried inside.

§

Dewey sighed with relief when he saw Amber disappear into the school. Phase one of their plan was complete. Now all he had to do was scoot around behind the gymnasium, stake out the side door, and wait until she emerged with the kid.

He turned around to go there, but before he could take two steps, he ran smack into . . . someone.

"Going somewhere?" a voice asked.

Stunned, Dewey looked up from where he had fallen onto his butt in the snow, his sunglasses having slipped down his nose. A dark figure was silhouetted by the lamplight in the snow-covered tennis court behind him. However, he didn't need his squinting eyes to tell him the source of that British accent.

"Clive? But how did you—"

"I'll ask the questions, if you don't mind." Clive grabbed Dewey by the elbow and yanked him to his feet. He pulled him in close, the steam from his breath huffing in Dewey's face. "For starters, where's Earl's case?"

§

Inside the gymnasium, "Waterloo" came to an end.

"Alright, ladies and gents, let's slow things down," the

DJ said. “It is Valentine’s Day, after all.” With that, the opening piano notes of “Total Eclipse of the Heart” by Bonnie Tyler rang through the gymnasium.

“Omigosh! I love this song too!” Joy said. “We have to dance it!” She went to pull Dean close, but he stiff-armed her, putting his hands on her shoulders.

“Oh no you don’t! I need to get back to my friends.”

“But Dean—”

Before she could finish, Dean took off, making a beeline toward the boys’ locker room, knowing Joy couldn’t follow him in there. However, just as he put his hand on the door to push it open, he spotted someone waving to him—a young woman whom he didn’t recognize. He looked around, making sure she wasn’t waving at someone else, then turned back to her as she approached.

“Are you Dean Muller?” Amber asked, having ditched her lousy accent.

“Yes, but who—”

“Amber Trickle, Yorkton Enterprise newspaper.” She shook his hand. “Do you have a bit of time to chat?”

Dean stared at her as his mind stumbled to figure out what was happening. “The Yorkton Enterprise? But why do you—”

“You are the person who headed up construction of that impressive snow maze just outside of town, aren’t you? The one on your mother’s land?”

“Oh, the snow maze. Well, I wouldn’t say I headed it up, but—”

“Excellent. We’re doing a story on it, and I wondered if you’d take like to step outside, so we can do a brief interview where it’s a little quieter!” She practically had to shout the last part in an effort to be heard over the music.

Dean looked around uncertainly, trying to spot a

chaperone. "Well, technically, we're not supposed to leave the gymnasium . . ."

"Oh, it's OK. I cleared it with the man at the front door."

"Mr. Peesker?"

Amber nodded. "Yes, that's his name."

"Well, if he said it's OK . . ." Dean looked around for the other boys. "But I wasn't the only one involved. You really should interview my friends too. Let me see if I—"

"Oh, we're going to interview all of you," Amber said quickly. "I just happened to find you first."

"Well, OK," Dean said, turning toward the front door. "As long as it's quick."

"Not that way," Amber said, turning him in the opposite direction. "My photographer is waiting outside the side entrance to take your picture, so it's less conspicuous. We want the newspaper story to be a surprise."

"Oh, good thinking," Dean said. Amber smiled to herself as she followed him down the dark hallway that led to the side door. Teenagers were so gullible.

§

"So, we're all agreed we should call the police?" Chad asked, looking at Andrew and Matt.

"Yes," Andrew replied.

"I guess so," Matt said. "But it's two against one. We need to find Dean and see what he thinks."

"But if he agrees with you, we'll just have a stalemate," Andrew pointed out.

Chad smirked at Andrew. "Do you really think Dean is going to side with Matt against us?"

Just then they spotted Joy walking through the crowd,

looking forlorn.

"Yo, Joy!"

Her eyes perked up at the sound of her name, but her face went glum again when she realized it was Matt and not Dean who had called out to her.

"What?"

"Have you seen Dean?"

"Yeah. The jerk just ditched me. He went off with another woman."

All three boys gaped at her. "Another woman?" Chad asked in disbelief.

She nodded vigorously, causing her tiara to wobble in her hair, the bobby pins that held it having come loose. "An older woman too."

"Joyce!" Matt exclaimed, smacking his fist into his palm. "Wait'll I—"

"No, an older woman," Joy said just as Matt's anger was ramping up. "An adult."

"Who?" Andrew asked.

Joy shrugged. "I don't know. I've never seen her before." With that she wandered off into the crowd, her head hanging.

The boys looked at one another. "Who could it be?" Chad asked.

"And where did they go?" Matt wondered, standing on his tiptoes and surveying the crowd.

Andrew shook his head. "I don't like the sound of this."

§

"Is this the right door?" Dean asked, glancing back at Amber.

She smiled sweetly. "Yes, that's the one."

Dean paused before opening it. "Are you sure about this? I mean, I feel kind of funny leaving the gymnasium with a complete stranger. And it's cold outside, not to mention snowing. Maybe I should get my—"

"Just open it!" Amber said, her anger flaring before she managed to tamp it back down again, forcing a pained smile. "Please. I'm sorry; my photographer and I are just anxious to get back to Yorkton as soon as possible tonight before the blizzard hits."

"There's seriously going to be a blizzard tonight?" Dean said. "Just our luck."

Sparks of mischief danced in Amber's eyes as Dean finally pushed on the bar that opened the door.

§

"Think we should make an announcement from the stage?" Chad asked as he, Matt, and Andrew pushed through the crowd, looking for Dean. "See if anyone's seen him?"

"No!" Matt replied. "I don't want to cause a panic."

"But if someone's gotten to Dean, this is exactly the time to panic!" Chad said.

"Hey, watch where you're going!" someone said as Matt shoved past him.

"Sorry!" Matt yelled over the music as he backed up, suddenly realizing he had stepped on someone's foot. He turned around to find Ben and Zoey glaring at him.

"Moo!" Ben said.

"Moo!" Zoey echoed, her hands on her hips. She was wearing a white dress with pink splotches on it, apparently to make her look like a jersey cow, and Ben was wearing a suit made out of the same material.

Matt rolled his eyes in disbelief and then turned back

to Chad. "Let's finish our circuit of the gym first. If we don't find him, then we can take things to the next level."

§

Outside the gym, Dean squinted as he looked around in the blowing snow. "Wow, you weren't kidding about a blizzard! How are we going to take a picture—" He stopped short when he saw a frightened look on Amber's face. "What's the matter?" Dean asked, raising his voice over the wind. "Do we have the wrong—"

"Hello, Amber," a voice with a British accent said. Dean followed her gaze as a dark figure stepped out of the shadows, his arm around another man's neck, holding him in a headlock. As Dean's mind struggled to process what he was seeing, one shape was unmistakable, even in the near darkness—an umbrella.

His mouth fell open. "No . . . not you!"

"I'm sorry, Amber," Dewey said. "I was about to come here when—"

"Shut up," Clive said, giving Dewey's neck a squeeze. Then he motioned to Amber and Dean with his other hand. "Both of you, come with me."

Dean swallowed hard and shivered from fear and the cold winter air. This was his first encounter with real-life criminals, and he was terrified. "But where are we . . . why are you . . . help!"

Dean turned to run, but Clive grabbed the back of his suit jacket, pulling him close, his other arm still wrapped around Dewey's neck. "If you know what's good for you, you better keep your mouth shut. This'll all be over quickly, kid. Now, just take us to that case."

Dean looked into Clive's eyes and swallowed hard, his

Adam's apple bobbing. "Would you believe we already turned it over to the police?"

Clive's upper lip curled. "You'd better hope not—for your sake."

Dean tried to swallow again, but his throat was way too dry.

§

After splitting up and searching the gymnasium, the locker room, and the school hallways, Matt, Andrew, and Chad regrouped on the balcony, so they could get a bird's eye view of the dance floor.

"It's like he just disappeared," Matt said, his eyes scanning the gyrating teens as they danced to "Addicted to Love" by Robert Palmer.

"Maybe he went home," Andrew suggested.

"Then who was that woman?" Chad asked.

"I think we should at least check outside," Matt said, heading for the stairs.

"If he did leave, he'll be long gone by now," Chad called after him.

"It still won't hurt to look!"

In the school foyer, the boys hurried past Mr. Peesker, who was seated at a table near the doors. "Leaving so soon?" he asked.

Matt paused, his hand on the door handle. "Oh, uh, we just had to go outside and check something."

"I'm sorry," Mr. Peesker said, standing up. "If you leave, you can't come back in."

"But we think our friend is in trouble out there. We just want to check on him."

Mr. Peesker shook his head. "I haven't seen anyone

leave, and I've been sitting here the entire time." The boys looked at one another. Maybe Dean was still in the school after all. "But I did see something strange out there tonight—at least I thought I did," Mr. Peesker continued, approaching the windows and peering outside.

"Oh yeah? What was that?" Matt asked.

Mr. Peesker laughed and shook his head. I don't know if it was the snow playing tricks on my eyes or what, but I could have sworn I saw a man silhouetted by the floodlight on the tennis court. And get this: he was holding an umbrella!"

The boys looked at each other one more time and then raced over and grabbed their snow gear from where they had left it hanging when they came in, then dashed for the front doors.

"Wait a second," Mr. Peesker said. "Where are you—"

The boys were gone before he could complete his question.

§

Clive dragged Dean and Dewey over to the New Yorker and then nodded to Amber. "The keys. They're in my right pocket."

"You should just let the kid go," Amber said as she dug into Clive's jacket pocket. "Shouldn't he Dewey?" She glared at him, nodding for him to answer.

"Yeah," Dewey said. "He already told us where to find the case."

"He could be lying," Clive replied. "Besides, he said it's in a snow maze. I don't have all night to crawl around looking for it."

"What are you going to do with us when you find it?"

Dewey asked as Amber unlocked the door.

"Wouldn't you like to know," Clive replied. He opened the back door and then motioned to Dewey and Dean. "Now get in."

Dean hesitated, staring into the back seat and wondering if he should call for help again or just do as he was told.

"Not so fast," a voice said.

Dean looked up in relief. Someone had seen them! His hope faded when his eyes were met by a big, imposing man with wavy salt-and-pepper hair, and he did not look happy. Dean glanced at his captors and realized they looked just as frightened as he felt.

"Earl!" Clive said, the first one who was able to find his voice. "You're right on time! In fact, I was just going to . . . wait a second, how did you find us?"

Earl held up one of Clive's posters and tapped the phone number at the bottom. "Tow truck driver tipped me off. Turns out he gave these two a ride, then saw one of your posters at the post office. You haven't been checking in, Clive. If I didn't know better, I'd say you were trying to double-cross me."

"No, Earl, honestly, I just wanted to surprise you. I—"

"Can it," Earl said. "I should have listened to my grandmother, God rest her soul. If you want a job done right, do it yourself." He crumpled up the poster and then glared at Dewey. "Hello, Mr. Biggs. Long time no see."

Dewey swallowed hard, too terrified to speak.

"Why do you always have to be such a bully, Earl?" Amber asked. "Just let us go. Your British bulldog here already knows where to find the case."

Earl sneered at her through the blowing snow. "You really think I'm going to leave a bunch of loose ends blowing around in the breeze like this? Now stop flapping your gums, and get in the car."

Amber crossed her arms in defiance. "Make me!"

"Hey, Dean! What are you doing with those people?"

They all turned to see Matt, Chad, and Andrew standing outside the school across the street.

"Help!" Dean cried. "They're kidnapping me!"

"Get in the car!" Earl ordered. "Now!" He grabbed Amber and shoved her into the back seat as she tried to punch, kick, and bite him, then got in behind her. Clive stuffed Dean in after Earl and then opened the driver's door and pushed Dewey in first, forcing him across the center console into the passenger seat.

"Give me the keys!" Clive shouted, holding his hand up and turning back to Amber. She stuck out her tongue and blew a wet raspberry at him, but Earl grabbed her hand and yanked it up, causing her to drop the keys into Clive's palm.

He shoved them into the ignition, only to be met by a familiar electronic voice. "A door is ajar. A door is . . ." He looked up and realized Dewey had quietly opened the passenger door and was trying to sneak out. "Nice try," Clive said, reaching across Dewey and slamming the door. Then he hit the button for the electric locks and fired up the car.

"They're getting away!" Matt shouted as the New Yorker pulled away from the curb, its tires spinning in the fresh snow.

"Let's get to the snowmobiles!" Andrew said, already putting on his helmet. They had ridden the snowmobiles to the dance, so they could go straight to the snow maze afterwards, and their parents wouldn't have to pick them up or drive them home. "We can get to the snow maze faster than they can if we go cross country."

"But what do we do when we get there?" Chad asked. "These people could be dangerous. They could have guns!"

The other boys paused, unsure what to do. If they didn't leave now, the criminals would get to the snow maze before they did, and then there was no telling what they would do with Dean once they got their hands on the case, but if the boys got there without any sort of backup, they could all be in trouble.

Just then a van came sliding around the corner where the street that passed by the school crossed Main Street. It fishtailed as the driver sought to regain control, then skidded to a stop right beside the boys, and the window rolled down.

"Mrs. Muller! Your timing is perfect!" Chad exclaimed.

She had a scowl on her face. "You boys know anything about a woman at this dance who's trying to pass herself off as my—Matt Taylor? Aren't you supposed to be sick in bed?"

"I feel a lot better now, Mrs. Muller. But we can talk about that—"

"You better not be thinking about coming to my snow maze tonight!"

"Actually, we're about to—"

"You need to call the police, Mrs. Muller," Andrew cut in, his face serious. "Dean is in trouble. He's been kidnapped. Tell the police to meet us at the snow maze as soon as possible." With that, he got onto his snowmobile and fired it up. Chad and Matt did the same on theirs.

"My Deanie? Kidnapped? Who would do such a thing?" Mrs. Muller shouted over the roar of the snow machines.

"Just call the RCMP!" Andrew said. "Now!"

With that, the two snowmobiles took off.

24

Snowbound

At Dr. Maharaj's house, Henrietta, Romanowski, Harpreet, and Gurvinder were about to dig in to a succulent meal of numerous Indian dishes, including shrimp korma, garlic naan, lamb curry, vegetable pakora, beef masala, palak paneer, daal, and mounds of basmati rice. All the food was laid out on the kitchen island, and everyone served themselves buffet style. The smells alone were enough to get Romanowski's mustache wiggling.

"You've really outdone yourself, Gurvinder," the staff sergeant said as he scooped some palak paneer, a green spinach-based dish with white chunks of cottage cheese in it, onto his rice. "This looks marvelous!"

"Thank you," Gurvinder said with a smile, "but you should direct your compliments to the chef, and it wasn't me!"

Romanowski looked up at Harpreet in surprise. "You cooked all this?"

The doctor grinned. "If someone didn't cook in this house, we'd starve!"

Gurvinder nudged his slight paunch. "It doesn't look like anyone is starving around here." They all had a good laugh at that.

Just then, Romanowski's pager went off. "Are you kidding me?" he exclaimed, looking down at it. "Tonight, of all nights?" He scowled as he read it, then set his plate on the counter.

"Richard, what is it?" Henrietta asked, looking at him with concern.

Romanowski glanced up at her and then at his hosts. "I'm sorry, but this sounds pretty serious."

They all followed him to the front door, where he grabbed his coat and hat. "The rest of you enjoy yourselves. I'll be back as soon as I can."

He gave Henrietta a quick kiss and then hurried out the door.

§

The snowmobiles roared across a frozen stubble field, their headlights barely strong enough to cut through the sheets of blowing snow, forcing the boys to slow down. The last thing they wanted to do was run into a barbed-wire fence or a rockpile.

"We'll never beat them there at this rate!" Matt said.

"Don't worry!" Andrew shouted. "This snow will force them to slow down too!" Despite the poor visibility, he squeezed the throttle a bit harder, causing the snowmobile to surge forward.

§

Clive leaned over the steering wheel, his windshield wipers and defrost fan on high as he struggled to see through the huge flakes streaming out of the darkness.

"Step on it!" Earl said.

"I'm going as fast as I dare," Clive replied.

"Keep an eye out for wildlife," Dewey warned. "This is exactly how I got into this situation in the first place."

"Shut up!" Earl shouted.

"But Earl," Dewey protested, "I was never going to keep the case for myself. I got in a car accident, and I couldn't remember—"

"I said shut up!"

"One more kilometer to go," Clive said as they passed one of Mrs. Muller's signs. "Good thing that crazy woman left us a breadcrumb trail."

A minute later, Clive skidded to a stop when they reached the turnoff to the road where the snow maze was located. They almost missed it, seeing as Mrs. Muller's sign at the corner had nearly been blown over by the wind. Clive backed up and then turned down the road, plowing through a snowdrift that had already begun to creep across the approach.

By the time they reached the snow maze site, the only indicator they were there was Mrs. Muller's final sign, which was flapping in the wind. Clive slammed the New Yorker into "park" and then opened his door. "Just give me a minute, and I'll—"

"Not so fast," Earl said.

Clive looked back at him, already halfway out the door. "But Earl, the kid says the case is in the maze. All we have to do is get it."

"Exactly," Earl said, opening his door. "We are going to get it. All of us. Together. Now move it." He motioned for Clive to unlock the doors, so the others could get out.

Once outside, they all stood there trying to see through the blowing flakes, the New Yorker's headlights cutting a pitiful swath through the wall of snow. "Which way, kid?" Earl asked, turning to Dean.

"Follow me," Dean said, his shoulders hunched and his entire body shivering from cold and fear. Just as he was about to trudge toward the tunnels, Earl grabbed his shoulder and shook his fist in Dean's face.

"And no tricks!"

Dean swallowed hard as he looked at Earl's hairy knuckles. "Yes, sir."

The others followed Dean through the snow, sinking up to their knees or further, none of them wearing snow boots or any other appropriate winter gear. When they reached one of the entrances to the maze, Dean stopped. "Here it is."

Earl looked around, his eyes full of suspicion. "What about those other tunnels?"

"They're just meant to throw people off," Dean said. "Three ways in, only one way out."

"You better be telling the truth, boy."

They were just about to crawl into the maze when they heard a shout. "Hey, Dumbo, over here!"

They looked up and saw Matt pop up and wave to them from another spot in the maze.

"No, over here!" Chad shouted, waving from yet another entrance.

"Don't look at them, look at me!" Andrew said, popping up in yet another spot.

Earl grabbed Dean's collar, his eyes simmering with anger. "Who are those punks? And I thought you said there was only one way out of this thing."

"Th-those are emergency exits," Dean said. "In case the maze collapses. And th-those guys . . . th-they're my f-friends."

"Then they're in a heap of trouble," Earl said, shoving Dean toward the tunnel. "Just like you." He turned to Dewey, Clive, and Amber. "You three, make yourselves useful and round up those kids."

"Yes, sir," Clive replied.

"Just do as the big man says," Dewey whispered to Amber when she stood rooted to the spot, her arms crossed. "You don't want him to hurt the kid, do you?"

She finally relented, the three of them splitting up and heading toward the various spots where the boys had popped up.

§

Romanowski's cruiser raced down the highway, siren on and emergency lights flashing, a plume of snow swirling in its wake.

In the passenger seat, Mrs. Muller gripped the door handle, her knuckles white with fear. "Can't this thing go any faster?"

Romanowski shot her an incredulous look. "I'm going as fast as I dare considering the weather conditions, ma'am."

"My Deanie's been kidnapped, and you're worried about a little snow? Step on it, sergeant!"

Romanowski grunted as he looked in his rearview mirror and saw the other cruiser close behind him, Chambers at the wheel and Rogers at his side for backup, then pressed on the accelerator.

§

Inside the snow maze, Earl followed Dean down the tunnel on his hands and knees and then nearly slammed his head into Dean's butt when he stopped short.

"What are you doing?" Earl growled. "Keep moving."

"I'm trying to remember which direction," Dean said.

"You built this thing, didn't you?"

"Yes, but only certain sections of it," Dean replied. "And we had headlamps."

"Well, make a decision," Earl said, holding up his cigarette lighter to reveal they were at the confluence of three tunnels. Dean finally chose the center tunnel, and Earl followed him.

Clive had trouble finding the spot where Chad had popped up until he happened to step on a spot in the snow that sounded hollow. He cleared the snow away and discovered one of the plywood emergency exits. He tore it off and then dove into the tunnel. He was just in time to spot Chad, who was wearing a headlamp, disappear around a corner.

"Get back here, you little chump!" Clive said, crawling after him.

Dewey had a similar experience as he pursued Andrew, following the glow of his headlamp.

"This is too easy," Dewey said. "Just give up!" he shouted, his voice dying almost instantly due to the insulating effect of the snow. "It's only a matter of time before we catch you!"

"How much farther?" Earl grunted, already breathing heavily from the uncustomary exertion.

"We're almost there," Dean said. He stopped beside the entrance to another tunnel. "It's right in there. Just wait here while I—"

"Not so fast," Earl said, slamming Dean against the tunnel wall with his elbow. He held up his lighter and shone it ahead, unable to see much beyond the entrance. He turned back to Dean. "Stay here," he said, shoving him against the wall for emphasis. "If you're not here when I come out, your friends are in a lot of trouble."

"Yes, sir," Dean said, happy for a moment's reprieve.

"How the heck do I get myself in these situations?" Amber complained as she crawled forward in the dark, the knees of her jeans soaked and her hands numb. "I'm going to kill you when we get out of here, Dewey!" she wailed. Just then she saw a glow up ahead. "Aha!" She scooted ahead to catch up to it.

Despite his speed, somehow Clive had lost track of Chad. Without a light, all he could do was crawl forward in the dark, hoping to stumble across him again. Suddenly, someone tackled him, pinning him to the floor of the tunnel.

"Gotcha!" Dewey cried.

"What the heck are you doing?" Clive bellowed when he realized who it was.

"Oh, sorry," Dewey said. "I thought—"

"I don't care what you thought," Clive exclaimed. "Just get off me!"

As they brushed the snow off themselves, Clive happened to spot a glow in the distance. "There they are!" he said. "Now come on, dipstick. Follow me."

When they emerged in the room where the light was, ready to pounce on whoever it was, instead of Chad or the other boys, they found Earl. He was holding his lighter up as he examined the rather large room in which they found themselves. Seconds later, Amber showed up from another tunnel, huffing from exertion. Earl looked at the others in disgust. "Are you telling me none of you managed to catch those kids?"

"It was dark, sir," Clive explained, "and we—"

"Where's the kid you had, Earl?" Amber said, one hand on her hip.

"He's right outside this room, if you must know," Earl replied. "Forget about them. Help me find that case!"

As the other three crawled into the room, Matt peeked around the corner of one of the tunnels and then looked back over his shoulder. "Now!"

A moment later, there was a loud whoomph, and Clive, Amber, Dewey, and Earl disappeared in an explosion of snow.

Across the room, crouching in another tunnel, Dean wiped his eyes and then looked up in surprise, realizing the room's roof was gone, the maze exposed to the open sky as snow continued to stream down, swirling in the wind. When he looked down, he had to choke back a laugh. Before him were Dewey, Clive, Amber, and Earl, all of them buried up to their chins in snow!

Earl glared up at him. "I'm going to kill you, you little brat!" He tried to move, but his arms were pinned to his sides, and he couldn't move his legs. He looked over at Clive. "Don't just sit there, get over here and help me!"

"I would, sir," Clive said, grunting with exertion as he tried to free himself, "but . . . I . . . can't . . . move!"

Just then, Matt appeared in another tunnel entrance, followed by Chad and Andrew in two other tunnels, all of them looking down at their captives. "Looking for something?" Matt asked, holding up the black hard-shell case.

"Why you little—" Earl's expletive was cut off by the sound of police sirens approaching. He redoubled his efforts to free himself. "Come on!" he said to the others.

"We've got to get out of here!"

"I just have one question before the police get here," Matt said as the sirens grew louder. "What kind of a dummy counterfeits two-dollar bills?"

Earl opened his mouth to offer one of the customary rebukes he reserved for wisecracking kids, but when he realized what Matt had said, he turned his head toward Dewey, who he could just see out of his peripheral vision. "Two-dollar bills? You stole printing plates for two-dollar bills? They were supposed to be twenty-dollar bills. Twenty!"

"But everyone counterfeits twenty-dollar bills," Dewey said. "I thought if we stuck to the two-dollar bills, no one would—"

"You thought?" Earl said. "Since when have I ever paid you to think? Tell me, when you were doing all this thinking, did it ever occur to you that it costs more than two dollars to counterfeit any bill no matter the denomination?"

"Uh, no sir," Dewey admitted.

"Not that it matters now," Earl grumbled as the sirens came to a stop, and they all saw red-and-blue lights flashing on the snow.

"I'm not officially with these guys!" Amber shouted as she struggled to free herself from the snow, hoping the police officers would hear her. "I was only trying to help them find Dewey!" Her eyes came to rest on Clive, who just happened to be stuck right in front of her, the two of them facing each other. "What are you looking at?" she griped.

"I'm sorry you got mixed up in this, Amber."

She glowered at Clive in disbelief. "You? Sorry? Pffft."

"I mean it. I admit I had my doubts about you at first—not to mention your eating habits—but I'll make sure the authorities know you got involved in this against your will."

“Well, I hope they throw the book at all of you. Especially you, Jeeves.”

Just then, Romanowski, Chambers, and Rogers appeared above, their guns drawn. “Alright, nobody move!” Romanowski shouted. “And put your hands up!”

“Uh, chief,” Chambers said as he took in the scene. “That last part may be a bit of a problem . . .”

25

Heroes

"Holiday hijinks in Milligan Creek last night led to the capture of some would-be counterfeiters and the recovery of some printing plates that had gone missing from the Canadian mint just over a week ago," Tucker Butker said as the newscast cut to footage of Matt, Chad, Andrew, Dean, and Mrs. Muller posing for a photograph alongside Constable Romanowski outside Milligan Creek Review newspaper office. "All thanks to an elaborate snow maze some local boys constructed on this landowner's property."

The newscast cut to Mrs. Muller showing a reporter around the remains of the snow maze and then stopping to face the camera as she responded to the reporter's question. "Are the boys heroes?" She shrugged. "Well, maybe some of them are, especially my son, Dean. But let me ask you a question: would we even be talking about them if I hadn't allowed them to build this snow maze on my land? I mean, how do you define the word 'hero' anyway?"

Matt turned down the volume on the TV, unable to handle any more of Mrs. Muller's attempt to redirect credit for the criminals' capture to herself. The boys had all gathered at the Taylors' house to watch it, having been told it would be the lead story on the evening news. They were recording it on their VCR, so they could watch the rest of it later.

"So how did you build that trapdoor anyway?" Dean asked, turning to Andrew.

"Yeah, and I still don't know how you found the time," Chad said.

"That collapsing roof was a nice touch too," Matt added. "How'd you pull it off?"

Andrew grinned and tapped his temple with his index finger. "Trade secret."

"Well, I'm just glad you did it," Dean said, "or things could have turned out a lot differently."

They all fell silent as they considered the possibilities.

"Next time we find anything like that, we're definitely calling the police, right Matt?" Chad said, giving his brother an imploring look.

"Yeah, I guess so," he replied. "It's great we caught those guys, but I'm still bummed we never got a chance to make any money off the maze."

"Well, I think you were really brave, Dean," Joyce said from the doorway. The boys all turned and looked at her. None of them realized she had been standing there.

Dean blushed with pride. "Thanks!"

"Don't encourage him," Matt muttered.

"Speaking of which, I think you owe Joy an apology—and a thank-you," Chad said.

"For what?" Dean asked.

"Without her, we never would have known you'd gone missing from the dance," Andrew said.

Dean nodded. "Oh yeah, right."

"You should get her some flowers," Joyce suggested. "Girls love flowers. Or maybe you could build her another snow sculpture."

Dean's mouth fell open. "But that snow sculpture, I didn't build it for her, I built it for—"

"Flowers are a great idea, Joyce," Matt said, clamping his hand over Dean's mouth. "We'll have Mrs. Bondar make up a doozy of a bouquet."

§

Nurse Chaykowski was filling out a report at the front desk of the Milligan Creek Hospital when she heard the front door open. Shortly thereafter, she was met by a blast of cold air that contained the typical smells that met her nose every time someone entered the hospital—a hint of pine trees, car exhaust, and a whiff of cologne. But what really got her attention was not the familiar smells but an unfamiliar scent that she rarely encountered inside the hospital: curry.

She looked up and saw Staff Sergeant Romanowski approaching her desk, a smile on his face and a large brown paper bag in his hand.

"Richard! To what do I owe the pleasure of your presence this morning?"

"Actually," he said as walked up and deposited the bag on the counter, "I'm the one who owes you."

She stood up and peeked into the bag. "Mmm . . . leftovers. Thank you so much!"

"And thank you for helping set up the perfect date. It's just too bad those criminals made a mess of things. But that's not why I brought you the food."

She looked up at him in surprise. "Oh, really? Then what's it for?"

"Remember when you promised to tell me how you

could tell the Maharaj brothers apart if I took you out to dinner?"

"Oh yeah, I forgot about that."

"Well, don't worry about it. There's no need."

She tilted her head and gave him a quizzical look. "Oh? Why not?"

"Let's just say that when I was over at Harpreet's house, I came up with my own system."

As if on cue, one of the doctors rounded the corner, scrutinizing a clipboard as he walked.

"If your system is so good," Nurse Chaykowski said, "let's see it in action."

"Watch and learn," Romanowski whispered, shooting a look at the doctor's flat stomach, "watch and learn." He put on a big smile. "Good morning, Bash!"

The doctor looked up from his clipboard and smiled. "Staff Sergeant Romanowski! So good to see you. Don't tell me you're here to interview another one of my patients."

"Nope," Romanowski replied, patting the paper bag. "Just making a delivery."

"Ah, yes," Bash said, leaning over the bag and inhaling deeply. "I thought I smelled something special. Of the two of us, my brother is the superior cook; I'll give him that."

"I heard that!" Harpreet said, sticking his head around the corner. "And don't you forget it."

The others all laughed.

"Well," Romanowski said as he turned to leave, "the good people of this country aren't paying me the big bucks to stand around yakking. Have a good day."

"You too, Staff Sergeant," Bash said, his nose already back in his clipboard.

"You'll have to share your secret with me sometime," Nurse Chaykowski called after him.

Romanowski paused in the doorway and smiled. "Come now, Sharon. Don't you know a true detective never reveals his secrets?"

§

Two weeks later, Clive, Dewey, and Earl were standing at attention alongside the other prisoners at the Saskatoon Provincial Correctional Center. It was visitors' day, and the warden was calling out the numbers of inmates who were lucky enough to have someone come see them.

All three men were awaiting their upcoming trials. Clive had been charged with kidnapping, as had Earl, who had also been charged with conspiracy to commit counterfeiting. Dewey had been charged with conspiracy to counterfeit, stealing the printing plates, mischief, stealing the license plates off the VW rabbit, driving an unregistered vehicle, and every other charge Romanowski could think to throw at him. The only good news was his concussion symptoms were finally fading, though the other prisoners kept stealing his sunglasses, and neither Earl nor Clive would do anything to protect him. Thus, he was forced to squint throughout their daily hour of exercise in the prison yard.

Once Amber told her side of the story, thanks to additional testimony from Clive, she had been released with no charges.

"Prisoner number 10542, please report to the visitation room," the warden said. Through the window, they saw Meinhardt waiting, a thermos in hand.

"Thank God," Earl said, stepping forward. "I'm not sure how much longer I could have lasted in here without a decent cup of tea."

Clive scoffed. "Meinhardt makes a decent cup of tea? Yeah right."

Earl looked back at him, his eyebrow raised. "As you said, there's nothing you did for me on a day-to-day basis that I couldn't train one of my monkeys to do in your place. And, well, if any of my men look like a monkey . . ." He nodded at Meinhardt, who smiled and waved as he saw Earl approach, seemingly with fewer teeth than before. "It's him."

Just then, they saw Amber enter the visitation room carrying a brown paper bag. Dewey rose up on the balls of his feet. "Oh, boy, I can't wait to see what she brought me." He could barely contain himself, already stepping forward as the warden made his next announcement.

"Prisoner number 10837, please report to the visitation room."

Dewey paused and looked down at the number on the breast pocket of his orange prison jumpsuit, then at Clive's, realizing the warden had just called out Clive's number. "Wait a second, I think there's been a mistake!"

"Step aside, little man," Clive said, pushing past him.

"And prisoner number 10832," the warden added.

"That's me!" Dewey said, hurrying after Clive. "Hey, wait up!"

When they got to the visitation room, Clive smiled as he and Dewey sat down at the table across from Amber. "So, to what do we owe the pleasure of your company?"

"Well, I was sitting at home yesterday thinking about you guys in prison, and something compelled me to put my hand to my forehead and ask, 'What would Dewey do?'"

"And?" Clive asked, casting a skeptical look at Dewey.

"And nothing. But it did occur to me that you might be lonely. And hungry." She pushed the paper bag across the table toward him.

Clive opened it and peeked inside. When he saw what it contained, he looked up at Amber and smiled. "Jimmy Dean! I should have guessed."

"Just a little thank-you for not dragging me down with the rest of you clowns."

Clive smirked as he pulled out a sausage-and-waffle breakfast stack, which was still warm from the microwave. "Don't think I wasn't tempted," he said as he tore open the plastic packaging with his teeth

"What about me?" Dewey asked, checking the paper bag and realizing it was empty.

In response, Amber pulled out a map of Saskatchewan and handed it to him. "Toburns obout mobaybobe ObI'm yobour soboul mobate obafter oball."

"Whobat dobo yobou mobean?" Dewey asked.

"ObI fobollobowed yobour clobues, oband obI fobound yobou."*

Clive looked at them in annoyance, his cheeks bulging with sausage and waffle. "Would you two knock it off with that stupid ob language?"

Just then, Dewey noticed a bulge in the map. He unfolded it and found a gold padlock inside. He looked up at Amber for an explanation.

"I cut our other lock off the bridge and replaced it with a padlock that matches this one," she said. "I figured we needed a fresh start. And this time I'm going to throw away the key." She held it up to show him.

Dewey swallowed hard. Like it or not, it looked like he was stuck with Amber for good. Then she pulled a second Jimmy Dean breakfast sandwich out of her coat

*To understand what they're saying, just take out the "obs."

pocket and tossed it to him. "Don't think I forgot about you," she said.

Dewey smiled. After weeks of prison food, the highly processed sodium-and-salt-infused sausage, egg, and cheese croissant seemed like a little piece of heaven. Maybe sticking with Amber wouldn't be so such a hardship after all . . .

A Brief Note on the Inspiration Behind This Book

This book was inspired by two experiences, one from my youth and one that occurred more recently.

One winter when I was a young teen, Foam Lake, Saskatchewan, received a huge amount of snow. That prompted a guy named Glenn Brown and some friends to excavate a huge snow maze on his property, which was in the gully carved out by Milligan Creek. Then they invited the church youth group to go through it one Friday night. We also excavated a huge snow cave, complete with bunk beds carved into the walls, and spent the night there. It's one of my fondest memories, even though I got terribly sick afterwards from sleeping in soaking wet clothes that night!

The second experience was driving across Saskatchewan a couple of years ago while doing writing workshops at various schools. Once again, the snow was thick, and in the ditches along the highway were all sorts of snowdrifts that were just begging to be tunneled into. All I could think was, *If only I had a shovel . . .*

That prompted another thought: what if some mysterious snow tunnels started appearing in Milligan Creek, and the boys set out to figure out who was digging them? If they found that person, who would it be? I noodled on that thought for a long time, eventually settling on someone who had lost something and was trying desperately to find it. However, it wasn't until several chapters into the book that I finally figured out what was in Dewey's hard-shell case!

In the end, the story took some turns I didn't expect, but that's what makes being an author exciting. I never know where inspiration will come from—or where it will lead.

About the Author

Kevin Miller grew up on a farm outside of Foam Lake, Saskatchewan, where he dreamed of becoming a writer. He got his first break as a newspaper reporter in Meadow Lake, SK. Within a year, he parlayed that into a job in book publishing, which eventually enabled him to become a full-time freelance writer and editor.

From there, Kevin transitioned into film, and he spent the next thirteen years traveling the world while working on a variety of feature films, documentaries, and short film projects. In addition to serving as a screenwriter, he has also worked as a director, producer, and film editor. These days, Kevin splits his time between writing, editing, filmmaking, and teaching.

When he's not working, he enjoys hanging out with his wife and four kids, fishing, hiking, canoeing, skiing, playing hockey, skateboarding, and otherwise exploring his world.

Kevin likes to talk about books, movies, and writing almost as much as he enjoys writing.

Also available in the Milligan Creek Series

Up the Creek!

When best friends Matt, Chad, Dean, and Andrew set out on a canoe trip down Milligan Creek during spring run-off season, little do they realize that their voyage through small-town Saskatchewan is about to turn into one of the wildest experiences of their lives—if they survive!

Unlimited

A school field trip to the local Wetlands Unlimited marsh just outside of Milligan Creek, SK, gives Matt, Chad, Dean, and Andrew a brilliant idea: hijacking the radio signal that transmits a recorded message about the marsh and using it to launch their own pirate radio station. Broadcasting late at night, mostly for their own amusement, their show quickly becomes an underground sensation. Keeping their identities a secret, the boys are ecstatic about the growing popularity of their program, until it draws the attention of Wetlands Unlimited—and the police!

The Water War

When a beautiful, mysterious new girl moves to Milligan Creek, everyone in town is so smitten that her mere presence threatens to ruin the perfect summer that Matt has planned for him, his brother, Chad, and their best friends, Andrew and Dean. So, the boys come up with what seems like the perfect distraction: a water war. It's the ultimate game of survival, where every player is both hunter and prey. But when Matt's buddies invite the new girl to join in, the game that was supposed to unite them against the interloper threatens to tear their close friendship apart.

The Great Grain Elevator Incident

When Milligan Creek's iconic grain elevators are slated for demolition, to be replaced by a huge, ugly cement-and-steel inland grain terminal a couple of miles from town, brothers Matt and Chad and their best friends Andrew and Dean concoct a wild scheme to save their grain elevators—and their small prairie community—from being wiped off the face of the planet.

Quiet on Set!

To celebrate their purchase of the old movie theater in Milligan Creek, the new owners launch a short film contest, complete with cash prizes and a chance to have the winning films screened at the theater's grand reopening. When word leaks out that a real Hollywood movie will be filming nearby, Matt and Chad Taylor and their best friends Andrew and Dean concoct an outrageous plan to make their short film the most spectacular of all by secretly taking advantage of everything the big-budget movie production has to offer, but only if they can pull it off without getting caught!

LARPers

When Matt accidentally causes the untimely death of Andrew's beloved Mages & Monsters character, he attempts to make it up to him by launching a live-action role-playing (LARP) version of the game. While the players set out on an epic adventure to free Milligan Creek from a fictional curse, fantasy and reality come crashing together in a way that could change the face of their small town forever!